Apocalypse Alice

a darker retelling

by

Melissa Volker

ISBN-13: 978-0-9997016-1-4

ISBN-10: 0-9997016-1-4

acknowledgements

Susan B., you are always a valuable second pair of eyes.

And always, Chris, you were the first to look, to challenge, and to force me to go deeper, darker and beyond what I thought I wanted. And you were right.

Chapters

Alice

No one starts out their lives a killer. No one wakes up in the morning and thinks, "I know -- I think I'll find out what it feels like to slash a blade across someone's gut until their insides are in my hands."

Nobody plans that kind of a life, to become something little more than a wild animal; to live, every day, on fight-or-flight instinct.

But sometimes you don't get to plan. Sometimes you don't get to choose.

Sometimes life happens, and instead of tea parties and fairy tales, it's tough shit, and you end up doing things you never -- and I mean *never* -- thought you were capable of doing.

Life is funny that way.

It can turn a page in a book you didn't even know you were reading and plunk you down in a story that was never supposed to be yours. But there you are. Alone. In charge. Having to grow up, get tough, savvy, but somehow -- and here's the kicker -- somehow hang on to some part of your humanity. And the pages are turning, and you better figure out your place fast or all those pages whipping by at lightning speed will tear you to shreds.

So I figured it out.

For me, that meant fashioning a combination shotgun-axe from discarded bits and slinging it across my back, always at the ready. It meant learning repairs, getting dirty, and standing taller than I felt until I felt it.

I figured it out for myself because I had to, and sometimes that meant the slash of a blade and bloody guts.

For the most part I've been okay with that.

As long as the guts weren't mine.

Stories

"Tell me again about The Downer…"

Alice was growing tired of sitting on the floor with her little sister, Lily, struggling to repair the generator -- again -- with spare parts she'd salvaged the day before. There was always so much to do.

Lily had a strange fascination with the stories of the harsh and forbidding lands beyond. She could have asked for the nicer stories -- those of the world before all this, lifetimes ago when it was…the opposite of what it was now. But she didn't ask for those. She asked for The Downer.

"Oh my god, Lily. Why?" Alice asked as she worked at a rusty bolt, the sweat dripping across her brow.

"Because I like scary stories!" The puckish eight-year-old rocked on her heels as she squatted beside her big

sister, her blue eyes wide and glimmering. She peered over Alice's shoulder at the tattered repair manual, scrunching up her face. Alice knew it was because there were no pictures and that meant 'boring'.

Lily wiped her nose on her sleeve. She looked like their father with his ghostly blue eyes and dirty blonde curls -- their only reminder of him, while Alice took after her mother with darker hair clipped short, and deep, brown eyes, faint splash of freckles, and small, lithe frame. To remember her, Alice had to look in the mirror because time was cruel, slowly stealing the clarity of her memories. She and Lily had been alone for a while.

Alice sighed but smiled, and took a rag to wipe Lily's nose. "What am I going to do with you, you ghoul?"

Lily grinned, coughed and crowed, "Tell me the story!"

Alice set down her wrench and wiped the sweat from her forehead with the back of her hand.

"Before The Fall, the world was different. Everywhere you looked you'd find blue skies, green grasses, rich, deep, cool pools of crystal water.

"Beyond what is now the Breach is a vast, seemingly endless land that was once like that -- a beautiful and rich valley full of wonder with lush, delicate plants and wildlife everywhere you looked. And at its center, the bustling city with glass towers and ivy-covered bricks rose into the sky, the streets packed with so many people you could almost lift your feet and be carried in their current.

"Everywhere you turned there were people, and sound, and noise; the world hummed with life.

"But after The Fall it was ravaged, the lush and delicate left decimated and faded, towers crumbled, glass shattered. And those who remained there grew wild, degenerate, dangerous. Anyone who wandered into The Downer did not return. Or, if they did, they were never the same.

"The Breach -- a thick, high, impenetrable wall -- was eventually built to seal them in and keep us out. To forever separate them from us."

Alice looked to her sister who sat, wide-eyed, her wan face full of intensity. Alice paused, thinking that was enough but Lily bounced on her heels. "Keep going!" she cried.

Alice smiled settling into the story, "Factions fought for control, each conflict bloodier and more brutal, until one faction reigned supreme. One that held control and has ruled for generations -- the Clan of Crimsa --

Lily leapt to her feet, interrupting, "Crimsa! She is powerful and evil..."

Alice laughed, "Yes, ruled by Crimsa, who lives in a huge citadel surrounded by another great wall But this one..." She paused in her work, leaning in close and lowering her voice, building the tension of her story.

"This wall is strewn with spikes on which the heads of her enemies are impaled, and is guarded by warriors who paint their faces red with enemy blood. She can be heard from the top of the parapets screaming, 'Heads will roll! Put them on a pike!' and she wears the dried heart of an enemy around her neck like a locket!" Alice lashed out as though to grab at Lily's chest, and the child screeched playfully and ran away.

Alice chased after her, but after one loop around the room, Lily stopped, halted by a fit of dry, raspy coughing.

"Okay...I think that's enough. We don't need any other reasons to have nightmares." Alice caught up to her and scooped Lily into her arms, wiping away smudges of dirt and grime from her face.

Yes, there were enough reasons for nightmares.

Choices

"**Lily! Get below -- now!**" Alice tried to send her sister down to the basement bunker while dashing around their small house, shuttering and boarding windows, and barricading the entrances. She set the trip wire on the front door, and placed a shock charger at the window.

Lily knew the drill but she still hesitated. Alice understood it was the constant fear that when she emerged again, more of her world would be irreparably changed.

It seemed to happen every time.

"LILY!" Alice shoved the bookcase sparsely stacked with scattered books, found objects and supplies that blocked the basement door out of the way and knelt down in front of her little sister. Lily fought a bout of rasping coughs and held her hands clasped to her ears against the approaching whoops and screeches; the sounds that filled everyone's nightmares.

At eight-years-old Lily was a decade younger than Alice and in spite of everything managed to retain the wide-eyed innocence and infuriating hope of a child who has never lost anything in her life. Even after having lost so very much.

"Dammit -- " Alice caught herself and softened. She straightened her sister's t-shirt -- as though that mattered, and adjusted the cuff on her pants. All futile gestures of normalcy. "Lily...c'mon... downstairs. You have to go. I'll be back soon. You'll be safe, and I'll be back..."

Lily met her with a fearful, disbelieving gaze discolored by a haze of anger. Then she threw her arms around Alice's neck, whispering, "Promise?"

"*Always*. On the light of the moon." Alice hugged her, feeling her small, thin body nearly vanish in her arms. Lily was the only one that ever made Alice feel anything soft. "Now *go*."

Lily reluctantly let go and slipped into the darkness behind the bookcase, her small lantern casting a weak glow around her as she descended the stairs. Alice paused, listening to her sister's thin breath trail off into the gloom. She rubbed her eyes, choked down the clench in her throat.

Once the bookcase was back in place, Alice grabbed her shotgun-axe and slung it over her shoulder, checked the cargo pockets of her pants for extra shells, and bolted out the back door -- making sure the screened frame closed slowly and quietly -- just in time to see a Rooker turning the corner and heading for her elderly neighbor. Down the gap between houses, overgrown with sweet-grass, its herbal aroma wafting into the heavy, thick air, she could just see old man Hellerman as he stood in his yard, guarding his front door.

Alice didn't know what he thought he was doing. She wanted to shout for him to get inside and take safe cover -- he was too old now to be standing his ground. But then again, maybe that was all he had left to do. None of them had much, and what they did have was theirs to fight for.

After a quick check around her, gauging her options, she ducked down and raced around the back of Hellerman's house. There, she shoved old storage boxes and tires up against the back of the small, one-story, faded blue bungalow, and clambered up to the low sloped roof.

Lying prone on the rough shingles she could stay out of view while looking beyond the dilapidated, patched up neighborhood they defiantly dubbed "The Gardens". A handful of residents stood guard around the rudimentary windmills that dotted the field behind the houses spun in the stale breeze, doing their best to generate power, as well as at the gardens nearby, and beyond them, more Rookers appeared over the rise. Adults and children alike, armed and wild, their figures appeared as a wavering mirage above the hot asphalt and quickly became silhouettes in the coming dusk. They leapt over debris, taking random swings at low hanging tree branches and crumbled fencing. They chanted, whooping into the air with a sound like a combination of a coyote howl and a dying rabbit. It was a big crew. A full raid. That hadn't happened in a while, and the calm had been -- pleasant.

Oddly, she disliked that there were children in the party. There was never a need to bring them on a raid. But then, that's why they did it. Most people hesitated to attack or defend against children, and that weakness gave Rookers the upper hand because their children were all but feral, and had no problem drawing blood.

The village defenders already stood at the border, ready to hold the line at the edge of their cul de sac against the approaching group.

Below she heard Hellerman grunt and choke out a "I have nothing. Nothing of value at all..." before his voice was reduced to a strangled gurgle. A few Rookers had come around and made their way in from the side.

Shit. This really was a full-on attack. Her thoughts flicked a moment to her house, hoping none had found their way there, hoping Lily stayed hidden, quiet. She needed to get back there. Defend her own.

Alice belly crawled along the roof to the front edge as she pulled her weapon from her back.

With a quick peek over the edge to locate her target, and without thought to his size or possible strength, she flipped herself over the side, landing on his shoulders, knocking him to the ground.

Before he had a moment to register her, the axe blade swung in a wide, pendulum arc, cutting through his chest, spraying her with blood. He cried out, raising his weapon but Alice reversed her swing, the butt of her shotgun catching him in the temple. She finished with a solid smash of the axe against his skull, ensuring he wasn't getting back up.

Ever.

The sounds of others engaging with incoming Rookers echoed down the street. Metal-on-metal, the grunts and raging of all out brawls. More were on the way. This raid was in full swing and it was getting darker by the second.

Alice's heart thundered, the thrum of her pulse whooshing in her ears, her breath drawing full and quick -- the adrenaline spun through her tightening muscles, heightening senses, making her battle ready.

She absently wiped at the blood splatter from her face and glanced quickly to the sky, the weak light of the moon trying to push through cloud cover.

The light of the moon.

A sound from her house -- wood breaking, pulse trap triggering with a *CRACK!*...

The air cut open with a shriek as the brush behind her crunched and snapped, and Alice whirled around to see a shadow lurching from the weeds near the house. On instinct alone she raised her shotgun and fired -- once, twice -- the blast echoing through the air, rising above the fray of voices at the border and blending with old man Hellerman's crying out, "Alice!"

But it was too late.

The lurching shadow fell at her feet, small, young, the chest slowly obliterated by a growing smear of dark red, the crooked body limp where it fell.

Lifeless.

Sometimes you don't get to choose.

Alice stood a moment, the moonlight burning a hole in the top of her head, sweat beading up and running trails through the blood on her face, the adrenaline spike bringing a wave of nausea.

Her weapon hung limp in her hand and she watched the world tunnel down as she became vaguely aware of the cacophonous sound of gunfire and metal clanging against metal swirling around her, just around the corner. The reverberation ebbed and flowed causing an illusion of motion to and fro, her body moving with it.

She swallowed hard, fighting the sense of her stomach turning in on itself. Someone went down with a grunt to her left, out in the street...

Someone calling her, *"Alice!"*

Her focus wavered, faltered, failed, her legs giving out beneath her.

After and Before

It was several days before Alice came around, but even once she did, something was left behind. A piece of her. She had always been tough, able, strong, defiant, but now a darkness hung draped around her shoulders as well; one she wore like a cloak and hood, moving in and around them, but keeping her distance. Where once she had to play at being adult but still managed to release the playful snarky teenager, she now fell serious, focused, withdrawn.

While the settlement worked to bury the dead and rebuild what had been destroyed, Alice corralled herself in her shed, stripping and repairing the motor bike she'd managed to keep hidden from the Rookers.

Not that it mattered. The thieves had taken their fuel cells and decimated their medical supplies, broken at least one windmill, and stole its battery.

While they had thankfully devised a well-hidden bunker, only keeping handy what they could afford to lose in a raid (as if they could afford to lose *anything*), Alice and the other Rummies would still have to go on a scavenge soon.

She tried to convince the elder members to let her take out a small party the day after she came to, but they balked, saying she needed more time. Nothing she said convinced them she was fine. It wasn't her fault Rookers brought kids on raids. It's just the way it is. And sometimes the way it is, is shit. But that's nothing new. That was life.

Having completed the bike repair, she sat on the dirt floor, wiped the sweat from her forehead, and reached for the water bottle behind her. Her throat had caked with the dry, rough, fine dirt that seemed to hang in the air around her, and the water ran cool down her throat.

Then she remembered -- she had a couple of fuel cells hidden in the house. Rookers don't usually spend a whole lot of time searching for shit. They ransack the obvious, grabbing what they can amid the fray of their victims fighting to defend themselves, and then move on. They are nomads, never pausing for long. Not even during a raid. There is a wildness to them, having left behind any desire for civilization. They are chaos in motion.

So while they might take a passing sweep through houses -- and she knew they had gone through hers because their radio was gone as was the food from the cooler -- they rarely went to other floors. The more time they spent in one place, the greater the chance of defeat. She did manage to take out one with the trip-wire she set. But that didn't stop another from carelessly stomping over her and taking what he could.

Leaving the shed, she scuffed across the back yard, slipping down her sunglasses as she emerged from the dusty dimness into the yellow light.

"Hey there, Alice," Old man Hellerman waved, pausing a moment in the repair of his rain barrel. "You doin' okay?" He was wiry, tall, his skin somehow both saggy and tight across his face at the same time, and he kept his hair buzzed to a gray, rough stubble.

He asked her the same thing every day since the raid.

Alice nodded her head, pausing a moment at the back door. "That thing can't be patched any more than it already is." She backtracked to the side of her shed and rolled out one in better condition, propping it beside him. "Here, take this one. Not worth trying to salvage that one anymore."

The old man looked down at his broken barrel, his shoulders slumping, and wiped the back of his hand across his cheek. "I guess you're right. I just...I hate..."

"I know," Alice replied, understanding how much people hated to finally let anything go. There was often so little, that even a beat up old rain barrel felt worth trying to salvage.

Alice was born after The Fall. While she'd heard stories from elders of what it had been like, she knew only *this*, the world around her -- a world of squandered and spent resources, collapsed economy and society, where famine and diseases took out so many, and where they had to scavenge, barter, hunt and steal what was needed.

And kill.

In the house she took the stairs two at a time, pausing outside Lily's room. A dull ache began behind her left eye, a remnant of where she knocked her head when she hit the ground defending the old man.

Alice scowled and grit her teeth. She didn't like thinking about that. *Knocked out.* Since when was she a liability in a fight? And it was, what, a week ago already?

She rubbed her eyes.

She knew Lily wasn't there at the moment, so she pushed the door open and stepped inside. It wasn't really even Lily's room. Lily didn't use it. Their father died just over a year ago, Lily never knew their mother -- she died giving birth to her.

So Alice and Lily slept in the same room. Lily felt safer, and Alice slept better knowing she was right there. But some of Lily's things were still stored there along with spare parts and other bits and pieces Alice brought home for them; including the ragamuffin bear made out of scraps and bits of animal fur.

Snatching it from the windowsill, Alice unbuttoned the back and slid her finger deep into the stuffing. Pulling them free, she held two, half full fuel cells in her hand.

The ache behind her eye grew sharper, more insistent, so she buttoned up the bear and turned to leave. But near the door she stopped. On the floor lay a book. *The* book. The one her father said was given to him by his parents, who got it from their parents. She knelt down and opened its loose board cover, her fingers tracing along the torn and taped pages. Pictures of things unimaginable filled it -- plants, animals, landscapes of color and incredible beauty, vast shores of sandy beaches; full of things that once had been but were now long gone, it served as a reminder of what was lost and a dream of what could be again. Lily loved that book and would sit for hours on end in Alice's lap marveling at the images of things both impossibly fantastic and still surprisingly familiar: "*Oh! Look at that! Imagine seeing that! And this -- this is growing across the street behind Jenny Alman's house!*"

Alice slammed the book shut and shoved it away. *Stories*, she thought. *Childish fairytales of a world long gone.*

Swallowing hard and pushing against the pain behind her eyes, she spun on her heels and headed back out to the shed.

Once the cells were in the bike, she grabbed her jacket and her pack, which she had already filled with water bags, food packs, extra ammunition, scrap detector, rags and a small pocket shovel. She slipped her shotgun-axe over her shoulder and pushed the bike out of the shed. Once on the road, Alice paused just a moment to glance at her tiny home that once hinted at being a bright sunny yellow but now, like so much, appeared tired (although Lily said it looked loved).

Lily. She thought of finding where she was and saying goodbye, but it only made it harder and often triggered a bout of coughing and upset, so instead

Alice just imagined her ruddy, dirt-smudged, crooked toothed smile, clenched her own jaw and headed around the corner to Max's.

Max was one of their settlement leaders. He wasn't the oldest, but he was smart, shrewd, tough and somehow still caring. At over six feet tall and stocky, he wasn't someone you'd pick a fight with, but he'd sooner crush you in an embrace than punch your teeth out.

But he could do both.

He was on the front porch of his brick and clapboard house, putting the last two nails in one of the stair treads he'd replaced. Alice stopped her bike at the crumbling walkway.

"Max -- I want to get the others and go..."

Max finished his work and then stood, turning toward her. He glanced at the murky sky, then back at Alice.

"Hello to you too, Alice. And yes, things are fine, thanks for asking..."

Alice rolled her eyes and forced a smile. A half a smile. She flattened her lips.

"We need stuff, Max. The market only provides so much, and, well, we need more to barter with. There's some handmade stuff still, and things from the garden, but -- "

"What about the bunker storage? That's got venison, and some medicinals, right?

Alice interrupted him, impatient. "Yes, *some*. The deer Jesse shot last week would have set us up for a while, but it wasn't in the bunker yet, and now it's gone.

"I don't want to wait until we're really desperate, Max. That's when people get stupid and careless and shit happens."

"Shit happens anyway, Alice, you know that -- " he stopped short, appearing to regret his words. He put the hammer down on the steps and sank his heavy frame beside it.

He squinted at her. Not because of the sun, but because it seemed to help him focus on her. See something beyond her small figure standing there, straddling her bike, both covered in a film of dirt and grease.

"Are you sure you're okay to go?"

Alice huffed, adjusted her sunglasses and ran her fingers through her sweat-stiff hair.

"Yes. Whatever. I'm fine. Except about people asking me if I'm okay. That's getting a bit old."

Max held his gaze on her and Alice softened. He had been much like a surrogate father to her.

"C'mon, Max. You know I'm right..." She smiled -- fully -- revealing the deep dimples in her cheeks, and one eyebrow cocking upward.

Max chuckled softly, his eyes sad, and he itched his eyebrow. "Well, I'm getting tired of you asking -- even though you aren't actually asking -- and tired of telling you to wait. If you're sure you are ready -- "

Before he could finish, Alice kicked on the bike and adjusted her pack. "I'll go get the others!" She shouted over the rumble of the engine. "We'll head to Tulgey Wood and the warehouses this time."

"That's too far, Alice!" Max tried.

"We're gonna have to!" she shouted over her shoulder. "I'll bring you back something nice!"

Max would have wished her luck -- which she didn't need, or told her to be careful -- which she already knew, but Alice was already gone, spinning the bike around in the opposite direction to go gather up the other Rummies.

Time to scavenge.

Through the Woods

Alice and three other rummies: Ryan, Mallory and Jae, headed out of The Gardens cul de sac and toward Tulgey Woods. Ryan and Mallory took the two-seater with the trailer wagon, which held Jae, the youngest of all of them. She was also the smallest -- quiet and able to crawl into places the rest of them couldn't, and fast. Alice had seen her jig and jag her way from the line of fire like a rabbit from a fox. She sat with her knit hat pulled down over her cropped hair, just a short, stray spray of blonde peeking out above her eye.

Cruising through empty streets and across a handful of vacant lots, they traversed terrain they'd been through hundreds of times, now picked clean of anything of value. After about fifteen minutes they reached a dead end and found themselves at the edge of the field surrounded by Tulgey Woods, a horseshoe patch of dense trees and brush that was the last patch of cover before the vast openness of scraggly fields -- the Barrens. They could just make out the Warehouses at the far end of the field beyond the tumble of sheds and other outbuildings scattered haphazardly about like stones thrown from a giant's hand.

Alice paused at the mouth of a narrow path across the field, one boot on the ground as her bike rumbled beneath her, and she adjusted her weapon across her back. She tugged on her jacket and made sure pockets were secure. Then she fingered the small, grubby, once-white, toy rabbit tucked under the straps on the shoulder of her jacket. The one Lily had given her on her last birthday. *"For scavenging!"* she had said.

"But I have the pebble you gave me in my pocket." Alice told her.

"That's to keep you safe. The rabbit is for finding things. He's good at sniffing stuff out."

Lily believed a lot in talismans and luck.

Lily believed in a lot of things.

Glancing to the others, she took a moment to wipe the dust from her sunglasses and licked her lips. She rubbed the muscles on the back of her neck and blinked away sweat from her eyes. She rolled her head in a futile attempt to ease the ache thrumming there. But that wasn't going anywhere.

Ryan removed his cap, swiped his hair back and replaced the cap in reverse, brim facing backward. He and Mallory both adjust the bags slung across their bodies and nodded.

The woods that ringed the field seem to loom higher, reaching up and out with each breath Alice took. There were spots where it spilled out into the field dangerously close to the overgrown path. They could try veering off it, but they weren't sure of the terrain, and the warehouses were almost a straight shot across.

"You okay, Alice?" Ryan called over the low rumble of their bikes.

Alice glanced over at the three of them, each one staring at her, waiting, a trio of eyes from blue to deep brown. The question made her check, and she was unhappy to find that her stomach clenched, her hands cramped and her mouth was dry. She was -- afraid -- of getting through these woods. And that pissed her off.

"I'm fine. Just -- weapons up and eyes open!"

The three nodded, they all checked that their trackers were functioning, signals strong and set as Alice took a deep breath swung her shotgun-axe in front of her, put the bike in gear and headed out.

The field was ragged, full of tall, overgrown grasses and shrubbery, the buildings alternately growing out of, or collapsing into the reeds and dirt.

She glanced behind her at the others who went a bit slower along the unfamiliar landscape.

Coming up on a curve where the woods oozed out into the grasses, the underbrush pushing against the reeds and the path winding around, they lost sight of the warehouses for just a moment, but Alice reminded herself they were just around the bend.

Almost there.

She wished the jitters would settle down.

As she came around the curve, Ryan and the others a short distance behind, Alice was pulled short by something lurching forward from the woods to her left. A figure dropped from the trees only steps away from her in the shaded brush. In a breath it leapt out of the thicket at her and without a thought she swung her shotgun and fired, the shadowed blur dropping to the ground.

The force threw her off balance as she tried to pick up speed, and Alice lost control of the bike as she cleared the corner of a small shed. The bike tipped onto its side in the weeds, and Alice rolled off a few yards from the tree line as Ryan sped by on the two-seater.

He pulled up and circled back, reaching her just as she lifted her bike up out of the grass.

"What the hell was that?" Ryan cried, cutting the engine.

Alice wiped at a scrape on her arm and worked to steady the staccato of her heart.

"What?" She and Ryan were good friends, but she didn't like the tone of his voice.

"That shot…what was it?"

"Someone came at me."

"Yeah, but did you see what? Or who? Animal or person?"

Alice dropped the stand on her bike and stood before Ryan and the others. "No. Why? What does it matter? Whatever it was came right at me."

Ryan dropped his head.

"What?!" Alice demanded

Mallory readjusted the wrap that held her long hair out of her face. "Well…maybe it was another scavenger. Maybe someone needed help. Or if it was an animal, maybe we could use it."

Alice stood a moment her pulse thundering in her ears, her teeth clenched. "Or maybe it was a Rooker. You want to go check? Be my guest!"

"Rookers usually don't travel alone." Mallory spoke softly.

The four of them stood a moment, each looking to the other, then Alice righted her bike, checked for damage, and climbed on.

"Alice -- " Ryan caught her before she started it up. "I'm sorry...I just -- "

Alice caught his gaze and wrestled with reflexive anger and adrenaline. She sighed. "I'm fine, Ryan. Really. But can we go? Standing out here doesn't make me any better."

"Sure. As soon as we check what that was. If it was an animal, we'll take it. If it's a Rooker, then something is off since there aren't any others..."

Alice knew there was more he was thinking but wasn't saying. She knew because in all honesty, she was thinking it, too. But what was she supposed to do? Wait until the thing was on top her? Wait to get a clear view of a Rooker barreling down on her with a double bladed pike ready to eviscerate her?

Not her guts.

But whatever they were all thinking didn't matter, because when they got to the edge of the woods they found it was, indeed, a Rooker -- female, older...and alone.

Jae flipped the woman over with the toe of her boot. "Why would she be out here alone?"

Alice shrugged. "Scout? Rogue?" She thought a moment and then looked to the group. "Maybe everyone is getting desperate."

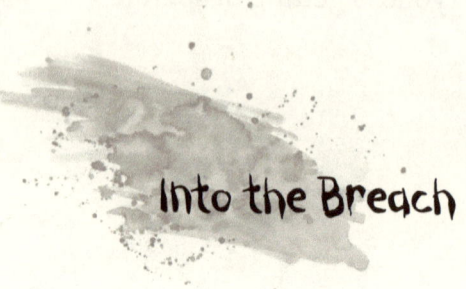

Into the Breach

Having finally reached the warehouses, the group got a solid couple of hours of scavenging in before all hell broke loose.

It started as a whistle carried on a breeze. Then the sound of metal against metal, and the thrashing of dried brush, or occasional whelp of some helpless animal. Then, the familiar figures emerged in the distance sending she and the others down into the reeds and behind battered walls.

Waiting.

They found the body of the old woman and their voices raised in feral rage. Alice dared a glance around the corner of half a shed wall to see just a glimpse of one of them, his face to the air, searching for scents like the animal he was.

Looking for *them*.

Now Alice raced through the tangled underbrush, between crumbling foundations, jagging around bushes and discarded scrap metal, her thoughts spinning, her lungs dry, the high-pitched, squelching whistles and screeches of the Rookers filling the late-afternoon air behind her.

Shit. Shit. Okay. Think. But even with her speed, her youth, right now Alice's mind fought to focus on her surroundings, finding options…surviving.

She was *not* going to lose what she'd recovered so far; they needed the cells and they needed the meds. This place was a goldmine. No way was she going to lose it all now.

"Now would be a good time for those good luck charms of yours to kick in, Lily…" Alice mumbled to herself, used to thinking out loud around her sister.

Taking a sharp turn she skidded on a patch of loose gravel, scraped her arm, ducked under a fallen log near the woods, and rolled into a slight gully where she lay flat and perfectly still, forcing her breath to grow shallow and quiet -- just as she'd been taught.

For one, brief moment she thought this might be it. Like Max said, it was a risk to come so far out., so close to the Barrens. Or to be out so early -- longer, lower shadows later in the day aided hiding. Unfortunately that was also the time the Rookers tended to move in force: dusk.

She also knew they didn't have much choice; supplies were running low and had been for a while. The recent raid just made that worse.

Her breath still came sharp, short, ragged. She closed her eyes, listening to the Rookers crash through the broken houses toward the tangle of woods, their boots smashing downed branches and kicking through metal, whistle signals and returns volleying back and forth. She focused on bringing her breathing down...slow...slow...

Her backpack and her shotgun dug into her back, but she ignored them both, just breathing... slow... slow...and in a few moments the screams and chatter echoed off into the distance.

If they had seen her, she lost them. She hoped the others could say the same.

Waiting several more minutes after the sounds had died out and the woods grew silent, Alice slowly emerged, climbing out of the gully and adjusting the load on her back.

She looked around. Listened. Stretched. Then let out a long, slow sigh, leaned against the log, and smoothed her sweaty, dusty, dark auburn hair out of her eyes.

"Way too close," she mumbled to herself.

Checking her watch, wiping at the additional scratches and dings on its surface, she carefully made her way back toward the warehouse field to find the other three. She considered going to check that her dirt bike remained hidden. She'd be sorely pissed if the Rookers had found it since she built that thing on her own.

Emerging from the woods, she inched her way between two storage sheds and into the open, pausing a moment to scan the space, finally seeing the others appear from their own protective cover. They each signaled quietly to one another and -- with a higher awareness of their surroundings -- went back to the task of finding something useful in what others had left behind.

Alice now tried to work fast. She quickly checked on her bike -- which was still there -- and went back to picking through what lay strewn about the field. They needed to grab what they could and start back. If one band of Rookers was out this way, there would probably be more. They were starting out earlier and earlier.

This was a pretty good spot with a lot discarded and left behind at the warehouses -- bits of machinery and remnants of tent fixtures and cookware -- but she found herself looking over her shoulder often, which slowed down her search. Nevertheless, her pack was filling -- scrapped gears, old fittings and hydraulics, and this trip she even found a dual-pack power cell, still nearly full.

Someone else must have dropped it in a rush because that's worth -- well, almost more than she owned. You don't leave those lying around.

It also meant they left in a hurry -- for a reason.

She checked her watch again. She really wanted to hit the huge, brick, three-story house in the middle of the far field. She could see bottom windows boarded up, but it didn't look like it was being used anymore. She also thought about how far they had to travel this time. Next time, it could be farther still.

But regardless of how far she was willing and able to go, pretty soon they might have to just pull up stakes and find somewhere else to live -- another run-down town or leftover neighborhood with closer places to scavenge -- if they could find one that hadn't been picked clean.

There had to be a place where they could do more than rummage through what others had left behind or lost. There had to still be places where they could create and build their own. Somewhere there ought to be pockets of resources that hadn't been totally laid to waste or thoroughly depleted.

Or, even, where it had begun to restore itself. Heal. The Earth did seem to do that over time: heal.

They had all worked hard to make their ramshackle encampment of houses safe, sturdy, comfortable. But now the surrounding areas were nearly picked clean of remnants worth scavenging.

She thought a moment. What if they *couldn't* find any place? What if everywhere had been used to dust and there was nothing left? What would happen on the day they discovered that everything everywhere had been used up?

Shaking that thought from her head, she returned to the task at hand. It was a big planet. There had to be more somewhere. It was just a matter of finding it.

She unconsciously adjusted her shotgun-axe across her back, a kind of security check to calm jittered nerves.

She stood a moment and stretched her back, adjusting her sunglasses as they slipped from sweat on the bridge of her nose in spite of a band keeping them on. Pulling a cloth from the pocket of her jacket, she dampened it with water from her pouch and rubbed her forehead, running her fingers through her hair.

There were dark clouds moving in fast over the trees. A turkey vulture soared lazily above the treetops, circling down, looking for cover.

If there was a storm coming, they needed to either start back now, or pick somewhere to wait it out. Judging by the speed of the front moving in, it would have to be the latter. Looked like the brick giant she'd wanted to explore might be it. It was on the other side of fields from where the Rookers came through, and had more lookout and cover options than warehouses and shacks.

They should have called it quits after the Rookers came. Nothing they found would matter if they didn't get it home.

She moved around into a position to signal the others that they ought to head for the building. Then she heard it: the whistles from the tree line along the far edge of the field. Were they doubling back? Or was this a new group?

Not that it mattered.

"What the hell?" Alice muttered to herself.

She froze, tipping her head to the sound, trying to distinguish the exact direction. Trying to separate echo from origin. She was girl, she was animal -- an extension of the world around her.

Then she saw them...just the tops of their heads, their scrap metal helmets gleaming in the flashes of sun winking through thickening skies, arms swinging blades and weapons as though loosening up, getting ready.

They were on foot -- but that didn't mean much, really. Somehow they always moved faster than it seemed they should be able. Particularly weighted down as they were with makeshift padding and gear. She guessed it was because they were always on the move, rarely staying in one place long. They were made to travel -- fast and far.

She glanced around quickly. She'd already moved far across the open expanse toward the brick building and the sheds and weeds were now too distant. There was nowhere to hide.

She was going to have to run.

But not the way she came; that's where they were coming from. She'd have to go around. If she really pushed, she might make it to a rocky outcropping, wait, and then go around behind them and grab her bike.

Looking up she caught her breath as she watched Jae leap up from a hiding hole beneath a pile of machinery and take off across the field.

But it was too late, the Rookers were too close and easily took her out in a couple of strides with a few monstrous swings of metal and sprays of blood.

Fuck!

Alice fought a sudden, unexpected surge of nausea and hoped the others stayed hidden.

She turned away, her pulse thrumming in her ears, her breath sharp and quick. Keeping low and trying to run parallel to them, she thought maybe she could make it around to the other side and circle behind them before they knew she was there. Her heart grew heavier, throwing itself against her rib cage.

They were coming fast.

And they had already spotted her.

"Shit. Sonofabitchshit." She scanned them quickly. A couple were small, maybe young boys -- or even girls. She could take those two if she had to, but not the three others. This wasn't a fight she could win.

So she turned and ran, her head spinning as she slid over the lip of a ravine in a little stretch of wooded area between broken, half sunken streets.

The sky closed in and the rains let go.

She slid and slipped, losing her grip, her sunglasses coming free and tumbling to her right as she landed at the bottom amid a small rush of bushes. Grabbing them quickly and slipping them into a cargo pocket -- they were a commodity of their own and had been her father's -- she ran forward again, hanging onto her pack while pulling her shotgun strap over her head.

She turned, seeing the Rookers at the top of the hill, little more than ragged silhouettes against the sky, the rain thrashing down around them. She paused just a moment and fired, hitting one of the larger members in the leg. He went down at the edge of the drop, tipping over the rim and sliding down through the mud a few yards away.

The others paused only a moment as Alice turned and ran on, sliding on muck, dodging brush and trees growing thick again, stumbling, her head colliding with a large, exposed root.

"Uhh -- " she grunted. Her vision wavered a moment and she fought a wave of nausea, but a rustle in the bushes to her left startled her, forcing her to focus. A child -- pale, a shock of white hair, light eyes, clothed head to toe in grubby white which quickly grew murky gray in the rain, shot her a panicked look before adjusting the rifle on his back, and racing head. Where had he come from?

Alice watched him pause and frantically tinker with something hanging around his neck while casting quick, furtive glances over his shoulder. She heard him mutter under his breath, "No no no. I need to get back..." as he peered toward the ground, shoving aside bushes and debris.

She ran toward him, seeing the air grow dark, dense, the rain blurring her vision.

How is it so dark up ahead?

Skidding to a halt, she went down on one knee. "Son of a bitch." It was the Breach. She didn't realize she was anywhere near it. Casting a quick glance, she noticed the wall rising up and out as far as she could see. It had been blocked by trees, the rain, her panic.

Turning again she saw the Rookers, who also saw the wall -- slowing to a walk down the small incline, sneering, readying their weapons. Probably figured they'd get a twofer. They might run fast, but they weren't ones to rush a kill. For that, they moved nice and slow.

They were fun that way.

One pulled what looked like an old flare gun off his back and got ready to aim. They knew she couldn't run the Breach and she had nowhere else to go.

Alice panicked, but looking back to the boy she realized he was fumbling with something in the ground. He knelt, taking the gadget from around his neck and placing it on the ground near his foot. She heard a crackle, metal grinding and a pop.

A door. A lock. In the ground.

40

So she had a choice -- sort of.

The Rookers stood, relishing their apparent victory, as the boy, partially hidden by low-lying brush, heaved back, lifting open a heavy, round, metal plate that swung up on a hinge.

Alice had to choose fast: Rookers or the Breach?

It was really a no-brainer. The devil she knew -- which would definitely kill her, the devil she didn't -- of which she knew only stories.

So as the flare gun slowly lowered, readying to explode a hole in her center, the Rookers whistling and squealing and growling in victory, Alice lurched toward the boy and threw herself against him, sending them both tumbling down.

She heard the blast of the flare gun behind her, something jarred her shoulder and her vision filled with a with a blinding flash of yellow and white light as the steel door slammed shut and the charge lock reset.

Then it was gone, and the world was nearly black, and she tumbled down a steep incline in a tunnel. A faint glow barely illuminated the space, but Alice couldn't tell from what, as she plunged, slipped, slid her way down, tree roots scraping and catching on her clothes, rocks jabbing into her side. She frantically dug her heels in, trying to slow her descent, get some control, faintly hearing the sound of the boy landing somewhere below with an "Ooph."

By the time Alice found herself at the bottom, disoriented and sore, her eyes had begun to adjust and she just noticed the boy hopping over what appeared to be old, half-buried tracks in the ground and rounding a curve.

Alice took a moment to try and orient herself, casting a furtive glance behind and above her toward the door she'd fallen through. There was no way to reach it again, and even so, it had locked behind them. Grabbing a flashlight she began her way along the tracks, her ankle sore, her pants torn at the knee.

She followed the curve she saw the boy take, and found at the end of another short stretch was a murky opening, the rain pummeling down beyond.

But the boy was gone.

"Shit, he's fast.." she thought to herself.

Plodding forward, she came out of the tunnel on the edge of a hill around a deep gully, runoff pooling around her and splashing over the sides.

As she took a step to get her bearings, her foot slipped in the mud and she went down again, this time down a muddy hill, sliding -- trying to grab passing roots and rocks as rain continued to hammer down but failing, things slick or too small to grasp. She tumbled sideways, losing her bearings, feeling the hill to be impossibly long, the fall unending until she landed, *SPLASH*, in a pool of murky, foul-smelling water.

Her heart racing, she splashed about, looking for a foothold, handhold, a moment of shock clouding her thinking.

After a few panicked moments in the water, she realized the pool was only waist high and she pushed herself to standing, rain cascading off her in sheets. She checked for injuries but found nothing beyond bruises and abrasions.

Her shoulder stung.

Standing in the shallows, out of the corner of her eye, she saw him, mud splattered and soaked, pulling himself to his feet and barreling through the barren trees to her left. He muttered something like, "...I took too long. She's gonna know..."

"Hey!" She called after him, trying to push her way through the muddy pool. The bottom was slick, thick, and she had to half swim toward the edge.

As she struggled through the downpour and sludge, an enormous rodent the size of a large dog appeared up out of the swampy water, nose twitching, webbed feet swatting hard at the surface as he paddled. Had it not inadvertently splashed in an effort to turn toward her, Alice may have ended up with a sizeable chunk out of her shoulder before realizing it was there.

Instead, she spun at the sound and dove for the shoreline, scrambling up into the tangle of overgrown brush, rolling onto her side while pulling her weapon free. Just as she landed on her back, the mutant beast lunged forward out of the water, its front teeth bared, its clawed toes outstretched, and as it came down on her, she swung wide with the axe end of her weapon, opening a gash on the creature's chest that splattered blood in all directions, mixing with the pummeling rain.

It landed on its side a few feet away, but scampered to its feet -- now wounded and angry -- and charged again. But Alice scrambled to standing, lowered her shotgun and fired. Once. Twice.

And the rat hit the ground with a thud.

Alice, panting and splattered in rat blood, crawled and slid to a nearby gathering of boulders. She leaned against them, her breathing heavy, her heart a steady, hard pounding in her chest.

"Jesus!" she exhaled, wiping her face with her sleeve. "Shit."

The rain abruptly waned, trickled, stopped, but the sky overhead remained murky and dim. Carefully nudging the rat with her toe to be sure it was, indeed, dead, she reloaded her shotgun and slung it back in place.

Far off in the distance, she heard a sound like a horn or some sort of blast of sound. It was faint, its echo pinging off the wall and the terrain around her.

Returning to the water, she used her rag to wash off the splatter from her face and neck.

She rubbed her arm where she had scraped it along the ground as she slid down, and rolled her shoulder which was stiff and sore.

She also quickly checked her pouch; she had long since taken to putting things like fuel cells and meds she found-- the important stuff -- into little sealed, plastic containers. She was happy to see all of it was fine.

Glancing back up to the drop she'd just taken she realized she wasn't going to get back home that way. The hill was slick with nothing to grab onto. Not to mention she needed a way through the locked and electrified door.

She thought about Lily. She thought about the other Rummies. She hoped they'd found shelter and she hoped the Rookers continued in the other direction.

She needed to find that boy. And his key.

But first, she needed to dry off and stay hidden. So rummaging through her pack for emergency supplies, she dug down to dry dirt, making a little divot, gathered some of the drier brush from under the nearby bushes, and lit a small fire.

Then she took off her boots, stretched her wet socks toward the crackling heat, and set out to wipe down her shotgun.

She ate a few of the nuts and dried berries in her pack, and looking around, tried to figure out where to go next.

Alone.

Beyond the Breach.

And there was no map of The Downer.

Chester

Before long her clothes had dried, at least enough to tolerate. She was used to varying degrees of discomfort.

Her weapon cleaned and ready, Alice packed up her emergency kit and stuffed it into a pocket of her jacket.

Spinning around on the rock, she scanned her surroundings. She had landed amid scrub trees and gravel in a deep ravine -- maybe a dry creek bed. Along the rise, the woods grew, lifting, rising higher, obscuring all but the top of the Breach, the gorge deep enough to nearly be a valley. The deep slope flanked her, merging in front of her with a collapsed overpass that seemed to lead into the outskirts of something. Beyond that, she couldn't tell for sure.

Misty, faint outlines of things hovered in the distance beyond ragged foliage, but all distorted. A fog had settled after the storm.

The stories of this place before The Fall seemed impossible; they were full of wonderful descriptions of rich tapestries of color, buildings tall and shining, and no end of plants, flowers, and animals running free. And people; all manner and type, bustling, busy... vibrant.

It was hard for Alice to imagine, looking at the desolate place it was now.

She sighed, unhappy about the fog. It wasn't thick, visibility distant, but there nevertheless. It was fog. It could hide things. Obscure them.

"Okay, Alice," she said to herself, "welcome to The Downer. Now, what do you do?

"Well," she answered herself, "I can't go back the way I came, so I supposed I'll head that way and look for the kid with the key." She faced the hill that went around the overpass just ahead of her.

Standing up, she adjusted her pack and her shotgun and started through the low-lying bushes and dried grasses.

She had a sudden moment of realizing how alone she was. No one ever traveled alone if they could help it. You learned that as soon as you could walk.

"Alright, Alice. Let's move. Too much in one place -- "

"Do you always talk to yourself?"

Alice whirled at the sound of the voice coming from behind her and to her left. She pulled her weapon free and aimed...somewhere.

But she hesitated.

"Woah -- no need to get defensive..." The voice emanated from up in the nearby trees, but scanning the branches she saw nothing. Except...

Except...

Staring into the shadows between limbs and amid tangled vines, she saw the leaves rustle and the branch rattle. As she watched, a figure slowly, so slowly, bled into view; a boy a few years younger than her, small, his blonde hair tousled and dirty. He perched on a tree limb, fidgeting with something on his wrist that looked like an overgrown, mutated wristwatch.

Alice watched with careful curiosity as the boy grew more solid and distinct.

Once fully visible, he broke out in an impossibly enormous grin and dropped out of the tree, landing softly, deftly to the ground. His giant, round glasses slightly distorted his eyes, and thin cables ran from the gadget on his wrist in a kind of network around his shoulders and chest. The jumpsuit he wore was streaked with oil and dirt stains forming scattered striations.

Waving his hand, he walked toward her, "Hey, I'm Chester. And if you're trying to figure out what to do next, let me suggest that you might want to get a move on and find someplace safe. And out of the way. And hidden."

Alice hesitated, glancing behind him and around the area for any more like him. She listened for sounds in the trees and the bushes -- for the sound of boots scuffing along gravel.

He read her expression. "Don't worry. It's just me. But it might not be for long." He gestured up the incline to the Breach. "You'll have set off the alarm smashing through the entry like that. The pylon hadn't fully deactivated. They pay attention. Crimsa's guards will be searching for whatever caused it...*who*ever."

Alice took a breath, trying to find what words she'd like to use first.

"I -- how did you -- ?" She motioned to the tree, referring to his prior invisibility.

He smiled again -- truly a huge smile for such a small face -- and held up his wrist with the enormous button and gauge-filled gadget strapped to it. "Like it? It's a holo-generator. Made it myself. Lets me cloak. That's how I get around safely. And unbothered. I don't like being bothered. Or monitored. Or known about, frankly." He stuck his hand out again. "Chester."

Alice couldn't help but laugh in spite of her strange and unsettling situation. It was an uncomfortable, unfamiliar sound.

She shook his hand. "Hi, Chester. I'm Alice."

She pointed to his holo-generator. "So -- does that just make you invisible, or does it work on that thing as well?" She motioned in the direction of the Breach.

Chester started walking toward the hill in the opposite direction, motioning for her to follow. She hesitantly trailed behind along the dry bed.

"No way," he answered. "Only the White One has access. At least as far as I know. He's the only one I've ever seen come and go."

"Figures," Alice muttered, kicking rocks and pebbles out of her way.

"So..." Chester began again, as though they were long-lost friends, "Are you an accidental or on purpose?" He glanced over his shoulder at her, pausing to let her catch up.

Alice shook her head, "I don't understand."

He paused, cocking one ear to the sky, then motioned for them to step off into the mass of rubble and debris just inside the woods at the edge of the rise. "There are two kinds that end up here: those who went through the Breach by accident somehow, and those who did on purpose."

Alice cleared her throat. The air there was sharp, metallic. "Well, by accident. Why the hell would anyone come on purpose?"

Chester paused and looked her in the eye, probing her honesty. "Well...for resources, of course. Or to stage a coup? Free the Downer?

"Although, I would hope there were more following behind if that was the case." Suddenly, his eyes lit up and he stepped in dropping his voice low, hushed. "Oh! Or are you some kind super soldier? I heard they existed...or did once. Or are you the first wave, just scoping it out?"

Alice had no idea what he was talking about. She ran her hands through her hair. "I -- what? No. I -- what resources? The Downer is a wasteland. Full of degenerates, insane --"

Chester had started walking again, but he stopped, turning on her. "It is? Is that what I am?"

Alice stared at him staring at her. "Isn't it?"

"Is that what they say now? Huh...boy stories change. A *lot*. Cuz that's not even close to the truth."

"So what's the truth?" Alice jogged to catch up with him while eyeing the nearby scrub brush.

Chester, scanning the space around him and checking off into the distance, apparently decided he didn't like dawdling and chatting, so he pulled Alice into the small thicket of washed out trees to the left of the crumpled beams of the overpass and guided her to sit on some unidentifiable rubble.

"The Downer is *not* a wasteland. Well -- this part is. A lot of it is, actually. Except for Crimsa's little kingdom -- well, not so little, really. Although...I think...I think that might..." He stumbled, halted, seemed to change his mind about continuing.

Alice rubbed her eyes and sighed. "I don't...I don't understand."

Chester squatted nearby and continued. "The story is that The Downer was once the last, great hope for us all to survive. After The Fall, as people scattered, various tribes formed, and explorers wandered, and it was found that there were tremendous resources beneath the surface here that had been lost or forgotten. Pockets to mine for fuel cells, underground springs. It was to be the place where we started over; where we planted, machined, rebuilt what was lost.

"But humans apparently do not learn well from past mistakes, and before long, they were fighting over what was here -- again.

"The Crimsa Clan was the strongest, Influencers from before The Fall with trained soldiers, mechanics, and more. They built a little kingdom, and within it, they create fuel cells, purify and pump water, grow food…it is apparently a paradise within those grisly walls. Has been, with rule passed down to the next in line. A veritable oligarchy. I don't even know which 'Crimsa' we are on anymore.

"Others work to mine and collect the raw materials needed and in return, they get a meager allotment of the bounty from her citadel and the 'privilege' of living somewhere in the Downer…

Alice held up her hand for him to stop. Her head was swimming. This was nothing like the stories she was told. "Is that what you do? Work for her?"

Chester stiffened, then grinned and shook his head. "Not me. I got *this*." He waggled his wrist at her. "I make myself scarce and live on my own."

"How? If Crimsa controls everything?"

Chester shrugged and smiled. "I'm creative. Resourceful. Inventive." He eyed her. "I make it work."

"And the Breach?"

Chester glanced to where she looked across the gorge to the top of the wall peaking through. "That? That was built to keep the rest of the world out. To keep out the scavengers looking to steal what she had. Or free those she'd enslaved. Or something. I think The Crimsa clan figured they could build their own little paradise here and the rest of the world could rot. Or, eventually, maybe she'd expand her empire. I dunno. Ancient history."

Alice couldn't believe it. She wanted to see this 'kingdom' for herself. If it was true...well...maybe this is what she was looking for. This was the answer for all of them.

"I need to get home. This was an accident. I was running from Rookers and got trapped. Through the Breach was my only option. But I can't go back that way..." She motioned back the way they came. "I need to find that kid and his gadget, key, whatever."

Chester thought a moment. "Well, across The Downer, is Crimsa's. That's where he'll be headed. But I'm not sure that's such a smart idea."

Alice scanned ahead of them but didn't see anything. "Well, do you have a better suggestion?"

Chester smiled and shrugged. "Nope. I do not. Aside from staying put."

Alice shook her head. "Yeah, that's not an option."

Chester just tipped his head in concession.

Alice looked around. "If it's so bad here under her rule, well, does anyone ever try to leave?"

Chester shook his head. "Not much anymore. Some believe it will kill them -- the Breach. They believe it's rigged to any unauthorized access. That's what they say, anyway. That the pylons are more than just security, but also a booby trap. Some believe it's worse out there -- at least here they have clean water, a roof over their heads, and food -- minimal as it all might be, and in spite of the conditions. They don't have to go looking for it.

"Plus, well…Crimsa. If she catches you -- " He stopped himself, apparently reconsidering what he was going to say. "Well, it's not pretty. And the guards not only protect her little paradise, they patrol the villages below, keeping a pretty close eye."

Alice was dumbfounded. This was not at all what she thought lay beyond the Breach. Not what anyone thought. It was supposed to be rife with wild, crazy, derelicts; overrun with those who were out of control, out of their minds. The Breach was to keep them *in*.

If that's not true…if there were raw materials, factories, filtration systems…if she could get word out… it could change everything.

All of a sudden the little boy in white burst out from behind them, bolting across the ravine toward the overpass.

Alice leapt to her feet to chase after him; he had access in and out of the Breach and was clearly headed somewhere now.

"Wait!" Chester called from his perch on the remains of an old wall.

"What?" Alice was impatient.

Chester thought a moment, as though trying to decide what to say, but then just shook his head. "If you are going after him you need to be careful. I'm serious. I don't use the holo-generator just because it's fun. Which it is, by the way."

He fished in his pocket. "Catch!" He tossed her a small, fabric pouch tied up with twine. Opening it, inside she found small, round, brass marbles. She held one up, noticing seams where it came together like flower petals. A small beam shot out a tiny hole, forming a wedge of light that scanned Alice head to toe before switching off.

She looked up at Chester, her eyes wide, questioning.

"Could come in handy if you get into trouble. Make sure you scan yourself with each one, then just throw them at the ground if you need a distraction!" he called.

She glanced over her shoulder to see the child in white clambering up a small hill, then turned back to Chester, eyebrows raised.

But before she could ask exactly what they'd do, he fiddled with the contraption on his wrist, let go with a toothy grin, and slowly, slowly vanished.

Tiny Alice

Alice sighed, shoved the pouch into her pants pocket and turned toward the hill. The child was disappearing over the top. Securing her pack and weapon, she raced behind him, leaping small rocks that loosed themselves in his ascent.

At the top, she stopped short. Over the rise on the other side lay a stretch of raised concrete -- a platform -- over which arched ornate metal latticework overgrown with vines. She realized what she thought was an overpass, was part of the platform that had collapsed into the gully.

Cracks ran like spiderwebs across the concrete, and off to either side lay broken, empty steel shells; long tubes, with rows of windows, and large openings revealing molded plastic seating within.

Old wires that had fallen from above lay strewn about like discarded party ribbon and stubborn weeds forced their way up between cracks and rusted holes.

Railcars. Old. Ones that once ran along tracks and beneath power lines, connecting all those people to all those places.

But the boy was gone -- vanished amid the steam rising from the post-rain heat, rocky outcroppings, half-standing station with its walls collapsing inward, and other ghostly, rusting remnants.

"Crap."

Alice glanced around and pulled the shotgun strap up over her head, slinging it over one shoulder, holding the weapon at the ready.

She carefully climbed over small boulders and concrete barriers, picked her way over an old, broken chain fence, peeked around the wrecked, oxidized walls, the foggy mist curling low along the ground.

A snake -- thick as her arm -- writhed in between a pile of rocks and iron bars. Farther away a pair of strange canines, their backs hunched, heads lowered, fur sparse, and eyes eerily aglow even in the daylight, shot her a wary look and trotted into the overgrowth.

It was otherworldly, really. A first glimpse into what the world might have been once. All the stories that had been handed down and passed on describing the world before The Fall, and the horror of losing it all, were just that to her -- stories. For Alice, the world had always been broken, lost, empty.

But here…here was a hint -- even a small one -- a peek into what the stories spoke of.

A sudden pop was quickly followed by a ping off the metal near her head and she dropped to the ground behind a rusting bench, ducking inside the nearest railcar door. Glancing in either direction, the series of cars locked together created a kind of lengthy hallway, each ending in crumpled, bent metal doors.

With a flurry, a small rush of birds burst out of the trees, scattering oddly in all directions, and she watched them disperse into the ruddy sky.

A second shot ricocheted nearby and she was able to judge the probable direction. Her father, the renaissance man who had been gentle, resourceful, strong; the man who taught her to shoot, to defend herself, navigate, and to help others in need -- who died doing just that -- had taught her well.

She missed him.

She missed a lot of people.

Lurching to her right she slid between two seats and reached the window. She peeked up over the edge and looked out.

Another shot, from the brush across the tracks beyond the other railcar, but she couldn't see anything clearly. Shadows grew longer, and she wasn't going to waste ammo without a clear target. Was it the boy? Or someone else? The guards Chester spoke of? Random denizen of the Downer? She didn't know.

Keeping low, she skittered through the car toward the next door, gingerly tipping one eye along the edge. She scanned the brush, the trees, cracked concrete barriers, and the inky deepness between.

There was nothing.

She carefully, slowly, stood and looked beyond the metal walls, but the brush remained still.

Alice sighed and rubbed her eyes. The sun slipped low in the sky, a bloody gash on the horizon, and she didn't want to travel at night. Already the sounds were changing as the light grew dim; the temperature dropped, the air began to fill with all manner of hoots and clicks and howls, and large bats dropped from their daytime hideouts to swoop overhead.

Wildlife was far more active here than where she lived. And perhaps more plentiful.

"Okay, Alice, while it's all very curious and fascinating, enough sight-seeing of this lovely land you've found yourself in…"

Not knowing what lay beyond she opted for the railcar for the night. Pushing herself into a corner with a clear view of the door but away from any windows, she drew her knees up to her chest, leaned against her pack, and with her gun across her lap she settled in for the night.

She took out the marbles from Chester and held each one aloft, allowing the emitted beam to scan her as the first one had, then carefully tucked them away. Whatever they were and whatever they did, she figured she should have them ready.

She tried to get some rest but it did not come easy. A tune from some far away memory trickled into her mind, and she hummed a few bars, completing it with, "Will you, won't you, will you, won't you, will you join the dance? Would not, could not, would not, could not, would not join the dance."

It was something her father used to sing to her and Lily as they fell asleep, trying to ignore the distant sounds of Rookers whining in the dark.

Odd that it came to her all of a sudden.

As darkness fell thick and black beneath a heavy, moonless sky, rustling and crunching sounds emerged from the surrounding area. She couldn't see anything, and didn't dare use a light and draw attention to herself, so she sat -- still, silent, listening, occasionally whispering quietly:

"Will you won't you..."

A snarl, a roar, the sound of metal drums being knocked over and rolling off the platform. A scuffle, a screech, the sound of predator and prey...

Will you, won't you...

...jaws locking down, bones breaking, a yelp...silence...

Will you join the dance?

...then, a carcass being dragged across the edge of the platform and down onto the ground, over grasses, gravel and into the surrounding brush.

Alice held her breath. Her jaw tight, trying to blend both in sight and smell into the metal around her, she was glad for the cover of darkness that hid whatever had just occurred.

Afterward, everything fell silent. Still. Every living thing retreating into the safety of shadows. Alice tried to close her eyes, drifting in and out of half-sleep, never quite surrendering, one ear to the world outside. The same way she'd slept for as long as she could remember.

Eventually, she did sleep for a stretch, waking to something sharp poking her wrist. Jolting up, she startled a large, colorful bird that had been pecking at her watch. It fluttered a few feet away, cocking its dark eye at her sideways.

Alice was mesmerized by the animal -- such a deep, iridescent blue with a slender neck, its head topped by a small spray of feathers. But it was the tail that rendered Alice breathless, loose and trailing, dragging behind the bird along the ground. When she shifted her weight to stretch, the bird hefted that tail into the air. The enormous feathers fanned out in an arc, each one topped with a blue and green eye-shape at the end.

Alice gasped. She had never seen anything so beautiful outside the Lily's book, and she imagined a world full of such creatures. The bird turned slow circles in front of her, its head darting about, its gigantic tail held aloft like a shield.

"Oh, Lily...you should see this..."

When Alice moved again, the bird fluttered and puffed and let out an unexpected sound -- a honking, squealing laugh of a sound that seemed more suited to a plumper, plainer, less impressive bird. Alice startled, then bristled.

"Are you laughing at me, you goofy bird? I bet you'd make good eating..."

As though it heard, the colorful creature suddenly flapped and fluttered a foot into the air and skittered out the door of the car, leaving one, lone tail feather behind on the ground.

Alice crawled forward to retrieve it and slid it through the straps on her pack. It waved like a small flag in the slight, stale breeze.

Fully awake, she rose and stretched, carefully peeking out the windows of the railcar. At the corner of the platform, splatter marks and fur served as evidence of the fight the previous night. It's a vision she'd seen before -- all that blood and destruction-- and she turned away before she imagined any more.

She checked the compass embedded in her watch and confirmed it with the location of the sun. It was past midday already, although it was hard to tell exactly as the sky never seemed to totally clear. It remained murky and yellow, the sun a dirty disk against a gray and brown sky. Nevertheless, she needed to get moving.

Carefully picking her away across the platform, she dropped over the edge, jogged across the broken tracks, over the bent fence on the other side, and into the woods beyond.

There were hints of old roadways -- overgrown, swallowed, the earth having shifted, sunk, or buckled -- building remnants poked up from pits in the earth or were slowly being consumed by surrounding foliage. Old brick and metal pieces spilled out across the roadways like the guts of an enormous beast, along with the occasional leftover carcass of a vehicle -- stray bits, and panels that had never been scavenged.

She kept her shotgun close, her pack pulled tightly to her back, and wandered around the desolate once-streets. Occasionally she'd hear strange sounds -- a huff of breath, scuffs on concrete -- but so far she hadn't come across any guards.

The houses were small -- what there was of them – many destroyed, vandalized, long-since abandoned.

Yet, so many others still had their slate shingled roofs with a small hole here and there, porches, while sloped and threatening, still standing as long as you watched for rotted stair boards; walls stood strong, windows mostly smashed, but frames intact, and while bushes and trees threatened to engulf, a few days of hacking back would take care of that. All of these seemed -- livable. In fact, they echoed of the life once inside, their defiance against decay seeming to scream that they had more to give.

Alice felt a squeeze in her heart. An actual ache that made her stop and take a deep breath.

A Home.

She could almost imagine Lily and other children squealing with laughter as they chased one another from porch, to shrubs, to yard.

But a scuffle and a huff behind her right shoulder dispelled the daydream. Then another a few degrees off. She pumped her shotgun and held it ready as she turned to see the pale face of the boy quickly pull back around the edge of a building. Was he watching her?

"Hey!" She stepped toward him just as two figures came forward from behind a derelict house.

As each stepped free of the shadows and debris they had hidden in, one in front of her now, the other to her left, she could see they were human -- but there was something off about them. Their clothes in tatters, hair matted and full of leaves and debris, their eyes resembled the canines she had passed earlier: wild, vicious -- feral. *This* is what she was told of The Downer.

They eyed her pack. Her water pouch. They hovered, never still, shifting their weight back and forth.

"Okay...look -- " Alice swung the barrel of her gun back and forth between them, each arc causing one of them to pause, to sniff the air and cock their head, their eyes never leaving her.

Alice continued to back away, but the two figures moved with her, step for step, occasionally skittering closer, then taking a step back.

She knew this dance...wild packs did it, the Rookers did it; they were sizing her up, looking for a weak spot.

Alice worked her whole life to not have a weak spot. She tried lurching toward them and while it startled them both and caused them to hesitate, it did not fully deter them and the dance began anew.

Join the dance... That probably wasn't what her father meant.

The one on her left was inching around to move behind her and the one in front picked up his pace. She didn't see any weapons, but that didn't mean they weren't hiding them somewhere.

They also looked a bit like they didn't necessarily need them -- bare hands and teeth can do just as much damage. Particularly if they are closer to beast than man.

And these two had beast written all over them.

"Okay, I don't have time for this."

Lowering her shotgun to the one in front just as he charged, she fired, aiming low and hitting him in the thigh. He went down with a howl -- guttural and feral -- which sent the female behind her into a rage. She came at Alice, her teeth bared, and fists raised.

Alice spun, swinging the axe head in a wide arc -- a clean, neck-severing cut. The woman stopped short, grabbing at her throat, stumbled backward and fell. Familiar sounds gurgled from her as the blood pooled around her head. In moments she fell unconscious. Shortly, she'd be dead.

The echo of the gunshots died out down the valley replaced by the howls of the guy on the ground, clutching his thigh, gnashing his teeth, and screaming a string of unintelligible words at her.

In the woods back toward the rail cars, Alice heard the rustling of branches and the snarling of predators waiting to stake an easy claim.

She grit her teeth, and with a brief, disgusted glance to the puddle of blood draining from the woman's neck, she turned, and ran, leaving the beasts in the woods to do as they liked.

I would not could not…

She took off down the street, taking a left, then a right, only slowing when the howling sounds finally abated.

She was breathless, sweating, and she took a quick pull on her water pouch, checking once behind her to be sure she hadn't been followed.

"Not a wasteland, huh?" she muttered through jagged breaths.

She sank onto the remnants of steps to a home no longer there and wiped the dirty sweat from her forehead.

From inside her shirt she pulled up a chain, on the end of which hung a small, plain stone wrapped in wire. Lily made it for her after their father died. She had picked it from in front of their house one night and sat for hours, her tiny, child's hands determined to wrap the thin wire around it, encasing it like a cage. Then she gave it to Alice and said it would protect her and she could never take it off. It was stupid, and meaningless, but Alice put it on and had been afraid to take it off ever since. And she was still here. So who knew? A wire-wrapped pebble and a dirty stuffed rabbit infused with the imaginary mojo of a child -- might be bunk, but both remained close.

But now it made her think of Lily, which made her think of the Breach, and the Rookers that forced her through it. She needed to get home.

"Shit..." She tucked the stone back inside her shirt and forced herself up. Adjusting her gear and cracking her neck, she looked around and picked a direction forward. It had grown quiet, the only sound being her boots scuffing along the pavement.

And then it wasn't. The only sound. Now after every step, she heard another, almost an echo of her own only snapping through bushes rather than scuffing on pavement.

She froze, then ducked to her right behind a a rusting decaying truck frame. She listened, hearing the sound again, along with the quiet chatter of voices.

One hand on her shotgun, she peered over the edge of the hood and saw a small, armor-clad cadre -- maybe six in all -- picking their way through a gap between buildings. They traveled in formation, sweeping an area before regrouping and changing direction.

Keeping out of view, she wasn't able to get a clear look, but with the armor and weapons ranging from rifles to pikes and staves, she ventured a guess: Crimsa's guards.

As they moved toward the road she crouched low, countering their path toward the truck. She was ready to slip round the rear as they passed the front, but at the last second they split -- three to one side, three to the other.

She had nowhere to go and steeled herself for the inevitable when, from back where she'd encountered the wild couple, there erupted an horrific howl followed by a flurry of snarling, barking, and the sound of something trouncing through the brambles.

"What the hell?" one of them exclaimed -- sounded female -- as all six of the guards froze, whirling in that direction.

In that moment, her movement muffled by whatever was happening in the woods, Alice rolled under the truck, yanking her pack quietly in after her.

The confrontation remained hidden behind toppled trees and crumbled foundations, escalating to a horrible frenzy of whines and snapping until they heard a yelp and then...nothing.

As in the gully hiding from the Rookers, Alice willed her breath to near silence.

"Jesus..." exhaled one of the guards, and the group shared nervous laughter before coming together on the far side of the truck.

If they were looking for her, they didn't seem terribly committed to the task.

Alice hunkered in place as she watched an enormous feline trot out of the bushes with a forearm and hand. It glanced around the area and leapt across the road, disappearing behind the buildings.

Once the area fell silent, save for the occasional buzz, yip, or chirp of critters in the woods, and the guards moved down a side street away from her, she carefully slipped from her spot, strapped on her gear, and continued on her way.

Turning a corner, the muddy sun sliding behind long, thin ribbons of gray clouds, she smelled something. A pungent, sweet odor wafted toward her from the partial rubble of a house nearby -- a gentle, flickering light emitting from the one remaining window, the last few shards barely hanging on.

She made her way quietly, keeping low, going around to the other side of the sunken porch to see if there was another window there, but they were boarded up.

While the building was damaged -- the front steps and entrance cracked, with bricks, stone, and siding strewn about -- it was overall in one piece.

And someone was inside.

She could only make out a shadowy image through the smudged and cracked glass near the door. There was one, small lantern inside, and the figure sat with its back to her, between the door and the lantern. Eerie shadows danced along the walls.

"You might as well come in," the figure said without moving from where it sat. It was a woman, her voice thin, cracked, old.

Alice froze, looking over her shoulder as though someone else might be there, but then turned back to the window.

"I'm talking to you. There's no one else here but the two of us."

The smell was dense now, making her heady, and hungry, and a little bit nauseous.

She moved to the doorway, which was covered by a tarp since the actual door lay shattered along the walkway in what may once have been a front yard.

Inside the air lay thick and heavy, what had been a hallway alongside a set of stairs was now just a large space, open to the room beyond -- only a few wall studs remaining. The woman sat on a large, round cushion, her back to Alice, facing a blank wall of peeling, patterned paper. Clothed in a tunic that had once been colorful and ornate, but was now drab and shabby, she sat perfectly still. Alice cautiously moved around the outer edges of the room, trying to peer around the woman and get a look. She skirted along the side wall lined with shelves holding small vials of seeds, dried leaves, and powder. She recognized many of the names as medicinal, others were foreign.

Reaching the front wall Alice faced a tall, slender, old woman, her gray hair well past her shoulders and braided with a red cord.

Her face showed her time here in long, thin, tributaries of lines, but her eyes were deep rich pools; there was beauty there still.

In front of her lay a long, wooden plank perched on old barrels on which sat a large bowl of something -- whatever she was smelling -- warm, spicy, sweet, earthy.

In her lap, the woman held a smaller bowl with a stubby grinding stone. Reaching into a box near her knee, she pulled out something brown, and dry and threw it into the grinder where she pummeled it to a powder.

"Who are you?" Alice finally asked when she found her voice. "If you don't mind me asking."

She may be in a wasteland, but she figured she didn't have to be rude.

The old woman paused in her work, raising her gaze to Alice, with one eye. "Who am I?"

Alice stared at the elder. "Yes… who are you?"

The woman thought a moment as though pondering, then ground a little more brown powder and put it into a cup. Then she picked up a nearby pot of steaming water that had been sitting on a small, makeshift stove Alice hadn't noticed, and poured it over the powder.

Instantly the room filled with that pungent, damp smell. It made Alice's eyes sting, and she put her hand to her nose.

The old woman held the steaming cup in the palms of her hands and stared at Alice. "I could ask you the same. And I will, but first -- " She took a long, slow sip, her movements fluid, sluggish; it made Alice tired just watching.

"To answer *your* question -- " the woman faltered, her gaze lifting as though the answer could be found on the ceiling. Then she stirred, her expression sparking to life, "I forget sometimes, but I believe the answer is there..." She pointed to an old piece of wood nailed to the wall.

Alice relaxed, feeling she was in little, if any danger, and turned to read the plaque.

Clarita Perl
Healer, counselor, practitioner of natural medicine.

"You're a healer?" Alice turned back to the old woman who sat with her eyes closed, breathing in the steam from the tea.

Opening just one eye she took another long, slow drink. "No. Not me. I am no one."

She suddenly appeared sad and Alice felt bad, thinking it might be her fault. Perhaps she had triggered unhappy memories. Probably not difficult to do. They all had unhappy memories. They were easy. It was the happy ones that were hard to find.

"Well, I'm Alice."

The old woman's head shot up, alert. "You are? Congratulations! Would you care for some soup? It's good for the soul -- full of earthy things like mushrooms and...other things. I forget sometimes." She motioned to the bowl as her eyes again drifted closed.

Alice ran her hands through her hair and stared suspiciously at Clarita -- if that was her name -- then the bowl, stepping a bit closer and taking a look at what was in it.

"Is that in it?" She pointed to her tea.

Clarita looked down at her cup, then back up at Alice and scoffed. "This? Well, no. Of course not. Who puts 'Kaverian Tea in soup? That's ridiculous."

Alice stared at the woman trying to figure out if she was crazy or just strange. She moved closer still to the pot of soup and sniffed the steam. While oddly sweet and spicy, she did not smell the same pungent odor as the tea. And smelling it made her realize how hungry she was for actual food. So she grabbed a nearby bowl and helped herself.

Keeping her gear on her, she sat on the floor a short distance away and carefully tasted the soup. Thick, aromatic, it filled her after just a few bites and she set the bowl back on the table.

Warm and sated, Alice grew drowsy and relaxed and leaned back against the wall while eyeing her host, feeling oddly content to just sit and rest. She knew she ought to get moving, knew she needed to get back to Lily, but for some reason felt she'd rather just...stay.

"So...do you live here alone?" Alice ventured, feeling she should try and make conversation.

Clarita glanced at her, or at least toward her, Alice couldn't be sure the old woman was actually focusing on her at all. In fact, she wasn't entirely certain the woman could see.

"We're all alone, aren't we child? In this world, while we share our space, we are -- ultimately -- alone."

Alice took a deep breath. Not quite the conversation she was hoping for. She was far too tired and distracted to be philosophical.

Clarita didn't seem to care whether or not they conversed. She just sat quietly, breathing in her tea, occasionally taking slow sips, keeping the cup held tightly in her hands.

They sat a long while in silence, and Alice thought she might have actually dozed off. She didn't really mind. It felt good to just...*be*.

But then she remembered. "Did you happen to see a boy -- in white...or do you know who he is?"

The old woman's eyes grew wide. "A boy?"

Alice nodded, hopeful.

"A boy…" Clarita breathed. "There *was* a boy…" Her voice grew wistful.

Alice leaned forward. "There was? Where did he go?"

Clarita's gaze grew distant, her voice sing-song, "There was a boy…a very strange enchanted boy…" She paused, looking down at her cup. "I heard that once. Someone used to sing it. My mother? My grandmother? Do *you* know?"

When she looked toward Alice again, her face grew wide, her mouth agape. She leaned forward on her cushion as though trying to get a better look, her face perplexed and inquisitive.

"How did you do that?"

Alice pulled herself a bit closer to the wall, trying to retreat from the woman's probing stare.

"How did I do what?" She looked left and right and back at the old woman.

"Get so…*small*…" Clarita peered intently at her, studying her with a gaze empty, but traveling up and down, her long, strangely lithe body leaning closer still.

Alice's brow furrowed and she shifted uncomfortably under the scrutiny; the attention stirred her focus, clearing the fog in her brain. "What?"

"So *small*...how did you do that? And getting smaller!"

At that point Clarita had leaned so far over, her tea sloshed from her cup, startling her, and Alice took the opportunity to scuttle from her spot and move back toward the door, away from the woman and whatever strangeness she was experiencing, grabbing a few vials from the shelves as she went.

Perhaps it was time to move on.

"Um...thanks for the -- food..." she stuttered.

"You didn't need to steal them, child," Clarita said without turning to see her. She just lift her cup to her mouth and drank. "You could have just asked for them. Although how you'll carry them while being so small is beyond me..."

Alice left the woman muttering to herself as she quickly checked the streets for obvious dangers, and slipped out onto the broken, shadowed sidewalks of late afternoon.

Monster Alice

Alice moved through the streets, the terrain growing dense, but with fewer buildings. Those that were there sat almost completely dismantled by time and abuse -- clapboard and wood rotting, splitting, leaving stone and brick behind. Greenery pushed its way up and through openings and encroached walkways.

She crept along, peering through dirty-smudged windows and holes in siding, finding nothing but barren broken shelves, long empty cabinets stripped of knobs and handles. Nothing of value left. Just corners with paper wasps and cubbies of nesting critters.

But no people.

As she turned a corner around an old storefront, the sign still hanging from one screw and swinging gently in the slightest breeze, the little boy in white -- appeared. Like a shooting star, he seemed to come from nowhere, streaking into view. He darted up and over rubble across the street, sped down the road close to the edge, and disappeared around another corner.

Alice snapped alert and followed, keeping low, with a watchful eye toward nearby, hidden sounds of skittering and scraping.

She could faintly hear the child chattering away to himself, although she only caught bits and pieces.

"...never should have stopped..."

"...just forget her..."

"...make up time..."

Turning the same corner, she saw him scramble up a small rise and hop a wrought iron fence, and without a thought to where it might lead, she did the same.

For a moment she lost him as she looked around. Broken stone archways stood to her right and left. Before her an old, rusted, hexagonal cage, its stone base nearly crumbled to dust, one side of the mesh bent and broken.

Turning a circle she realized there were more enclosures in various states of decay and disrepair, and barely recognizable paths that meandered around and in between. The overgrowth throughout was thick and dense, unfamiliar sounds coming from unseen places.

Branches shuttered and rustled, rocks tumbled, something slid across the ground; but whatever made the sounds remained hidden from sight.

Alice held her shotgun ready, having no interest in being caught unprepared by either human or animal.

As she made her way around the center enclosure, she came across an old, broken panel on the ground that still held faint, barely-there lettering. All she could make out was: ZOO.

She nudged the sign with her boot, the sound of it shifting along the ground startling something out of the trees.

Her peripheral vision caught a flash of white, and she turned just in time to see the boy cast a quick glance her way and duck through a broken area in the fence across the courtyard.

Alice sprang after him, straight across the cobblestone. She had to crawl through the fence hole, careful not to get caught on her pack, and slid down the hill on the opposite side.

At the bottom, she found herself on another street. This one wider, large cracks and gaps tearing through the surface, the grass at the edges encroaching, blurring the line between road and woods. Light poles rose sporadically around the area, stretching into the sky, floodlights on top casting down a sickly illumination across arcs of land.

The boy, however, was nowhere.

How did he do that?

Stepping out into the middle of the roadway she looked down in each direction. She was exposed, no trees or buildings on either side, just a long stretch of open boulevard. Ahead of her a flood light cut through the dingy air to what looked like an overpass. Behind her, a ramp lead down into a stretch of burned out field and old foundations.

Through the haze in the distance, she could just make out a couple of pylons off to her right -- Breach relays where there was an electrical field for extra protection. Before that though lay a spate of hills, and broken neighborhoods, and the edges of a small city.

Behind it all there seemed a layer of thick, smoky haze full of a faint, amber glow.

She wondered…*Crimsa's*?

She needed to get out of the unprotected open and find a place to hole up for the night, so she headed down the ramp.

At the base the stanchions were covered in graffiti, and an old, yellow bus sat, alone, strung with strings of colorful flags. Old torches lay strewn about, and a small sapling grew up against the side, nearly embedded in the metal.

Scanning the area, eyeing the shadows in and around the overpass supports, she made her way to the bus and peered inside the door windows. Her boot kicked a pile of trash near the front wheel and instantly enormous, toothy jaws lunged toward the door, the dog snarling and snapping but unable to do much more than scrape angrily at the frame. Alice fell backward to the pavement, but quickly scrambled to her feet. She circled the bus, the dog's hoarse barks heard from within, but saw no one else around. Was it left there or did it get trapped by accident?

At the back she studied the hatch door. A long, large, handle stuck out against a rusty latch. She tried pulling it down, but it only scraped slightly and stuck. She heard the dog scamper from the front of the bus and begin digging against the back door, its nails clacking like pebbles against the steel.

It wasn't her problem, and the damned thing would have taken her face off if the front door wasn't jammed shut, but she couldn't bring herself to just leave the thing there. It would die.

"Shit. Alright, pooch…might wanna back off a bit."

Pulling out her weapon, she turned the butt of the axe forward and held it like a baseball bat. Then she took aim and swung as hard as she could at the handle. It collided solidly, the reverberation jolting her wrists and she dropped the shotgun on the ground.

"Son of a bitch!"

The dog stopped barking.

Rubbing her wrists and stretching her arms she retrieved her weapon and took a stronger stance. Rather than a full on swing this time, she pulled up a bit, taking several smaller, more focused whacks until she saw the lever move.

Two more and it popped free.

"Okay," she spoke to the dog as though it would understand, her tone light and friendly. "You ready to get out, bud? I'm gonna open the door..."

Slinging her weapon back over her shoulder she grabbed the handle and pulled the rest of the way down. The latch released, and, keeping herself hidden behind the door, she pulled it open.

She didn't have to go far before she heard a yip, and the scraggly mutt leapt to the ground and took off like a shot, quickly vanishing into rubble at the edge of the underpass.

"You're welcome!" Alice hollered after it.

Glancing into the bus she noticed the remnants of something -- a rabbit? -- beneath a seat. As she turned, two figures half tumbled, half ran down a small incline behind one the stanchions and stumbled into the clearing. Alice spun, pressing her back against the bus and raising her weapon as the two untangled themselves and got to their feet, no yet noticing Alice

One was a young woman, her hair long, full -- a bushy swath around her head, her muscular arms ending in large, mitt-covered hands. She swung wildly at her companion -- a young man -- lithe, swift, and wearing some sort of makeshift helmet on his head with a single, stumpy horn on its front. He swung a short sword limply in front of him, which the young woman swatted out of the way.

"You severely suck at this, Eins." The girl taunted, as she smacked the small blade away from her, sending her partner stumbling backward.

"Maybe if you stopped cheating, Ari, it'd be a fair game!" He shouted back, scooting around another stanchion and using it as sheild.

Alice watched a moment until she determined they weren't a threat, and seemed only to be engaged in their own mock-adventure, then turned to slip around the other side of the bus and away. But her axe clanged against the metal, the sound pinging loudly.

Alice froze, and the two travelers stopped mid parry.

"Woah! Look at that!" The young woman named Ari tossed her tousled mane of dirty blonde hair out of her eyes and worked the mitts from her hands as she strode toward the bus.

Her partner, Eins, tripped once and then jogged up behind her, the two eyeing Alice, the bus, and Alice again.

"Is this yours?" Eins asked her, pointing toward the bus with the tip of his blade?

Alice stood rigid, pulling herself tall, and shook her head. "Nope. Just let a trapped dog out."

"Cuz we'll happily fight you for it," Ari stepped menacingly toward Alice, the mitts gripped in her right hand. Although she didn't seem committed to the gesture. While Alice guessed they were several years older than her, they also weren't really used to fighting. It was play.

Alice shook her head and stepped away. "No need. It's all yours. I was just leaving."

Eins and Ari exchanged a wary, uncertain, and perhaps slightly disappointed glance and then broke into gapped, toothy grins and ran around to the back to climb in.

Alice left them there, chattering to one another, "Eeww...there's a dead rabbit...", "So clear it out...", "Why me? You clear it out...", "Jesus, Eins, your such a baby...", as she turned and made her back out from under the overpass.

As she came through the brush to the street she heard a voice behind her, "Have you eaten something? You've been traveling a while with a long way yet to go if you're going where I think you are..."

Spinning on her heels, Alice watched Chester slowly come into view where he walked along the edge of a retaining wall. At the end, he jumped off and met her on the road.

"Jesus -- " she cried, "You oughta rethink your entrances there, Chester. One of these days someone might just take a shot at you."

Chester waved her off, smiling, seemingly unconcerned about anything like that happening. He walked a bit away from her, weaving in and out of iron beams that held up the old overhang to an empty energy station.

"So -- did you?"

"Did I what?" Alice had forgotten what they were talking about, as she was scanning the area for the little boy in white.

"Eat? Have you eaten?"

"Oh, yeah, " she briefly turned her attention to him. "Yeah. Some old woman in a building a ways back..."

Chester nodded. "Long hair? Seriously smelly tea?"

Alice laughed, "Yes! That's her. What is with that stuff?"

Chester's smile dropped. While it never vanished completely, it took on a different hue, "Yeah, Clarita. Well...she's been here forever... seriously -- I have no idea how old she is except that she's old enough to remember a better time. Maybe not before The Fall -- because she won't talk about it -- but certainly before *this*.

"Not sure she remembers anymore, though. That stuff she drinks kinda takes care of that."

Now Alice felt bad for slipping out of there so quickly. "Oh. That's actually kind of sad."

You never can tell a person's story.

Except that most of them are probably sad.

She fished out her water bottle, took a drink, then offered it to Chester. But he declined.

Just beyond the end of the ramp and down the road, Alice grew incredibly tired.

Like, seriously exhausted.

Feet-dragging, eye-drooping, couldn't-see-straight tired.

Chester noticed. "Hey, Alice -- you okay?"

Alice paused, stifling a yawn and trying to shake off the numbing fatigue. "I don't know. I just got crazy tired.

Chester smirked. "Probably Clarita. Betting there was something in whatever you ate."

Alice threw up her hands. "Seriously? Goddamit! I *asked* her!"

Chester stopped. "What did you ask her?"

Alice had trouble focusing. "What? I...um..." she huffed, stifled a yawn. "I asked if any of her tea was in the stew."

Chester blew out a laugh. "Yeah...wrong question...should have asked if there was *anything* in that stew -- other than food."

Alice rubbed her face, scowling. "Are you freaking kidding me? She drugged me?"

Chester shook his head. "Nah. Probably just some herbs or something. Nothing horrible. But she likes to stay mellow -- because...you know...trying to forget and all..."

Alice rolled her eyes and fought sleep. "Great."

"Here -- " Chester motioned to the station behind them. As the sky darkened and rain began to fall again, one of the streetlights that loomed overhead cast a garish glow that spilled through broken windows creating misshapen, crooked shadows.

Alice followed him in, crossing the room past old shelving and trash, all the way to the back and away from the front windows where she backed into the corner, slowly sliding down to the floor. "If I ever see Clarita again, I'll..." She faded, Chester's dopey, grinning face the last thing she saw before her eyes slowly, slowly drifted closed.

She is sitting on the floor of a room, a lantern chasing away the dreariness. Her father sits beside her, carefully balancing cards against one another; first three, then a few more perpendicular to those, continuing on until he has a criss-cross set upon which he lays cards flat, like a roof.

He continues on to the next level, repeating the pattern, young Alice marveling at how simple, flimsy playing cards could be stacked in such a way as to create a seemingly sturdy structure.

Until baby Lily crawls by, grabbing at a bottom card that formed an outer wall. With one, quick movement, the entire structure collapses to the ground to the delightful squeals of baby Lily....

...Screeches and whistles and hollers fill the dank, smoky air. Trying to breathe she finds it thick, rancid, stinging her nose and her throat.

She scrambles blindly, reaching out with her hands, flailing into the smoky mess toward another sound...

"ALICE!" Sobbing, crying, whimpering...Lily calls for her somewhere in the dark.

Footsteps. Clanging. Metal against wood.

"Girls -- RUN!" Her father, pushing them forward, away...

Screeching, crying, whistling --

"ALICE!"

LILY!

Alice woke abruptly, grabbed by the strap of her pack and yanked to her feet while she was still groggy and incoherent.

She stumbled, landing sharply on her knee, sending a jolt up into her hip, just as she felt her gun strap wrenched over her head, twisting her shoulder.

That woke her completely up.

"What the -- "She pulled herself straight, her eyes adjusting to the daylight and focusing on four men clad in rough, but finished metal chest plates, shoulder guards, shin guards, and metal gauntlets on their arms.

Each carried a rifle.

She twisted against a steely grip as they yelled at her, pulling her back and forth, and she struggled to stay standing. She saw the red smears across their chest plates -- blood smudged into the shapes of hearts.

Crimsa's guards.

Different ones from the six the day before.

Each also wore a helmet with a visor that dipped down over their eyes, red blotches of dried blood wiped across their cheeks. And on their faces, at the top of their cheekbones near their left eye: a scar tattoo in the shape of a heart.

"Who are you?"

Alice didn't answer, just stood still, stiff.

The one who had hold of her spun her roughly, and shoved her into the wall, her cheek striking hard, snapping her head back. Her vision blurred a moment, but she shook free when she felt him snatch her pack from her back.

"Hey!" She jerked her arm free of his and stood her ground, eyeing him squarely. Her head rang with the force of the blow against the wall but she fought hard to stay alert.

While the guard took one step back, he had the muzzle of a rifle lowered squarely at her chest. "I asked you who you are and what you are doing in The Downer."

The other three stood silently nearby shifting their feet. She took a moment to scan her surroundings, taking note of windows, doorways, nearby shelving. To her left in the wall behind her was what appeared to be an opening toward a back exit.

She raised her hands, smiling. "Okay. We seem to have gotten off on the wrong foot. But you did scare the shit out of me since I was sound asleep."

"Who are you?" repeated the one with the muzzle leveled at her heart. It was apparently all he could think of to say.

She eyed them all again, trying to stall, her mind racing. She also had the beginnings of a headache behind her eyes and her cheek stung.

Her weapon lay at the guard's feet, right beside her bag. Not far, but too far to make a lunge for.

"My name is Alice. And you?" She smiled again. "Never mind. I know -- you are Crimsa's guards, right?" She gestured carefully toward the hearts on their armor. "I'm a little confused. What did I do? Is this building off limits? I didn't notice a sign or anything...what makes you think I'm not from here, anyway?"

Instead of answering, the guard stepped forward again and grabbed her arm, clearly intending to restrain her.

Alice took a breath and dropped all her weight to the ground, knocking the guard off balance. From the floor, she swung out her foot and took out his legs, and he crashed to his side near her.

In that moment, she grabbed for her bag and her gun, yanking them closer, but the other guards all raised their weapons, freezing her in place.

The guard on the floor had the wind knocked out of him but was slowly recovering. When he sat up, he looked at her and backhanded her across the face, opening a gash on her temple.

She fought the urge to cry out, instead, just returned to sitting, wincing just a little, and wiped away a bit of blood with the back of her hand. Her cheek stung and throbbed.

Scanning from one to the other she had to admit defeat. There was no way she could take them all. They had protective gear, weapons, and there were more of them.

But then she remembered.

Again, raising her hands as if to show compliance and cooperation, she gestured to her pocket. "Okay -- I give. I'll show you why I'm here. Who I am. But I have to get into this pocket, okay?"

The guards exchanged a look, and the one she had knocked to the ground motioned for another to come forward and retrieve whatever it was. He seemed to hesitate a moment, looking to the other guards, then tentatively stepped forward.

"Oh, okay...gonna get it yourself. That's fine. Just be nice..."

She never broke her gaze with the guard who reached into her cargo pocket and retrieved the small, drawstring pouch. He held it out for the leader to see.

They all looked at it silently.

She rolled her eyes. "Well, you have to open it. Want me to do it?" She started to reach forward, but three guns lowered on her. "Okay…that's fine…Go ahead. You do it."

Alice flicked her gaze toward the doorway behind her, gauging the distance to it. The guard with the pouch leaned his weapon against the wall and carefully opened the bag, tipping out two brass marbles.

Alice put on her proud, "isn't that cool" face. The leader scowled.

"What is this?" he demanded.

Alice shrugged. "Well, hard to explain, actually. So I should just show you."

A dog outside let out a howling bark, the guard holding the marbles glancing quickly toward the sound.

In that instant, with all the force she could muster, she swung her hand up under his arm, sending the marbles into the air. As the guards watched them, she grabbed her gear and bolted for the back door. She hoped they did something when they hit the ground, otherwise, she'd have some choice words for Chester.

"Halt!" the leader cried, and she heard all weapons click and lock.

She skid to a stop and turned toward them, now several feet away in a vestibule by the back door. The marbles hit the floor in front of the guards and burst open. She backed further away as a blue mist erupted from each of the marbles, wafting up into the faces of the guards. Each in turn, they dropped their guns and covered their faces, shielding their eyes, coughing, fumbling.

Panicked, they looked up again as out of each marble grew a monstrous version of Alice -- so tall their heads scraped against the ceiling. They appeared mechanical, and yet insubstantial -- distorted and holographic -- but anything they touched sparked, smoldered and incinerated to ash as though torched by a huge electrical charge.

From the dark of the back room, she watched the two electric Alices disrupting shelves, burning holes in plaster. They stomped and stumbled toward the guards, causing them to snatch at their weapons and scatter, their eyes still tearing from the mist. They collided and bumped into each other, one of them stumbling accidentally into a giant Alice. Her hand reached down to his head, and taking firm hold, his helmet immediately smoldered, turning white hot and melting to his skull. He screamed and fought, but the Alice held firm, charring his head, his shoulders, a burning electrical charge racing through his body like blue strings.

In all the chaos, the real Alice turned and ran.

The Grotto Mole

The benefit of an overgrown, wild world of rubble is that there are plenty of places to duck and cover.

Although judging by the sounds behind her, the effects of the Alice marbles might last a while. A few gunshots and desperate screams made her wonder if any of them would make it out alive.

That was answered as a few seconds later an enormous explosion rocked the ground, a shockwave buffeted her, and she turned to see a billow of fiery smoke roiling into the sky.

Guess not.

She watched a moment as the flames leapt and spun a sooty mass of clouds. Ash and debris rained down, small bits making it as far as where she stood. It was somewhat satisfying, although a small part of her tried not to dwell too long on the images of searing, electrically charged guards, and as the fire slowly consumed the building, Alice turned away and moved on. Wandering around the area, the streets were puddled from the rain; an amalgam of dirt, metallic dust, ground concrete. Vehicle husks lay scattered about -- hollow, empty shells picked clean; large trucks and their empty containers lay tipped and scattered like a child's toys.

Her arm was sore from being twisted and her cheek hurt where it hit the wall. She could feel it beginning to bruise and swell, as well as the spot on her jaw where she'd been struck.

Settling onto a hunk of concrete she took a moment to just rest, pulling the lucky rabbit from the strap on her jacket, fingering its ears and tiny, round eyes. Her breath caught on something sharp in her chest and she winced.

"Oh, Lily...I hope the Hammond boys are being nice, and if they aren't, I hope you kick their asses. And I hope you hang in there until I get home. I'm sorry I didn't see you before I left." She realized she was talking to herself and looked around, taking a long, slow breath. Something nagged at her. She felt dizzy and nauseous and like she was forgetting something.

She hurt. She was tired. She needed to get home.

Hungry, she, jammed the lucky rabbit back beneath the straps and rummaged through her pack for a hunk of bread and some dried meat. She never set out scavenging without a moderate supply of food because she never knew how long she'd be gone. Tough to hike around all day without refueling.

It wasn't enough, but it would do for now. But she was going to need to find some food somewhere at some point. She wished Chester was around. He always seemed to have something to help her out.

She rolled her head, trying to release the tension in her neck, checked that nothing had been taken from her pack by the guards, made sure her gun was loaded, and then stood, trying to determine where to go next.

To her left stood a large, concrete block building -- maybe old storage? Across the street sat a rusted out trailer, old neon lights smashed and broken, just the letters D,N,E and half an R remained. On the ground in front, a warped piece of plywood with the words "Keep Out" slopped in faded paint. Beyond that a few vacant lots and then buildings grew denser again, brick facades, several stories mixed with lower storefronts and lots.

She loaded her gear and headed toward the trailer. Standing on tiptoe she could just peek through one of the cracked windows to see a dilapidated counter, some broken chairs.

Approaching the boarded up door, she leaned back and gave it a sharp kick with her boot. The old wood easily cracked and gave way, and after knocking out additional boards, she stepped inside.

The air hung foul and rank, dashing any hopes of finding some kind of food or something useful. But a sound around the counter toward the back caught her attention. Hanging onto her gun she crept around the edge of the counter and was about to move toward the back room when a snarl accompanied a dark shape colliding with her chest and knocking her to the ground.

"Ooph, hell..." was all she could get out as the enormous dog knocked the wind out of her. Her shotgun between herself and the animal, she kept the animal's snapping jaws from her face as she pushed against it and brought her legs up and around its chest.

With a sharp wrench she rolled them both over and was about to put a shell into the dog's side when she heard, "Nah!"

The dog froze and scampered back where he came just as the whistle of something flying by

Alice's head put a makeshift arrow into the wall across from her.

Whirling around with her weapon held high, she found herself face to face with two girls maybe a few years older than Lily. Reminiscent of the vagrant wilders she had come across earlier, their eyes glared with viciousness and untamed fury, as they stood side-by-side -- sentries to their tiny realm. One, her face long and thin, limbs gangly and angled, jut her chin out sharply sending her lower lip up and out in a defiant pout, while the other, smaller, rounder more reserved, stood deadpan, dark, large eyes fixed vacantly on her.

Alice sank back, keeping her weapon ready, but praying she wouldn't have to use it on them. Just the thought caused the world before her to waver as though underwater, her thoughts clogged and cloudy, her stomach lurching over.

While another arrow sat primed in the bow, the dog crouched beside the other, neither girl made a move toward her. They stood, like footmen to the empty eatery. Alice never turned her back on either one, simply slipped quietly backward toward the door and scrambled outside.

She made her way toward the other building, glancing at the faint image of bulky monoliths through the haze in the distance. There always seemed to be steam, or smoke wafting into the air above.

Something moved in the corner of her eye.

Turning, she saw the boy -- just a glimpse of his white pants vanishing into a hole near the side of the building she hadn't noticed before.

Jogging up to it she saw the ground had collapsed, opening a sinkhole, and the boy had ducked into a tunnel, beneath the building, and under the hill.

Securing her gear, she scuttled along the edge, finding small footholds, and then dropped down into the tunnel.

It got dark fairly quickly so she pulled out her flashlight, shining it down the length of the corridor. She just caught a burst of white as the boy turned left at a corner.

Alice jogged after him, finding another tunnel that led straight, the boy about halfway down, scurrying as fast as his little legs would carry him, the rifle clacking against his back.

She thought of calling out to him but considered it might spook him into turning and firing. This was too small a space to have a gun fight.

The tunnel they were in curved left, and then around that curve were two corridors to choose from.

The boy had already gone down one and she wasn't sure which.

"Great." Alice huffed and rubbed her forehead, nicking the spot on her temple where she'd been hit earlier. She winced.

She flashed her light down each, but couldn't see anything. However, she did hear a scuffling sound down the one on the right. Hoping it was the boy, she followed.

The corridor opened quite wide and appeared to have been excavated more than the others. She passed a small opening on her right and cautiously shined her light in. It appeared to be a room of some kind -- not large, and without much in it. Just a pile in the corner that looked like bedding.

It lay empty.

Continuing on she found a few more like that, some with blankets and bedding, others containing things like locked chests, baskets (some kind of dried fruit, to which she helped herself), and various possessions, although she had no idea to whom they belonged. The boy perhaps? Hideaways, or layovers for long journeys? But there were several rooms and just one of him. At each one she paused, wondering who used them, what kind of people lived beneath the ground?

Eventually, the hall led to an opening; a kind of underground grotto full of a gentle, glowing light from a small hole up above. The air appeared misty, full of tiny sparkles.

The boy was already on the far side, rounding a stone pillar, and heading up an incline to an exit on the other side.

At the back, the wall was partially collapsed, the rubble on top of a stretch of railway track. That's when she noticed the rest of the track, which ran straight through the pool, curved, and ran up the incline the boy had taken to the exit.

In the corner lay a partly buried train car, and next to the grotto an empty wooden cart sat waiting on the tracks.

But Alice's attention was ultimately drawn to a man at the edge of the pool in the middle of the grotto. An odd sight, he was squat, round with an unexpectedly narrow face for his size and stature. Wearing a makeshift helmet with some kind of respirator protruding from over his mouth and nose, and a circular shield worn on his back like an armored shell, he reminded Alice of a somewhat misshapen, cobbled together man-turtle

He sat on the ground, working at something he had in his lap, sniffling and wiping at his eyes as though he was crying.

Alice slipped on a pile of rocks, drawing his attention. He snapped his head toward her, squinting, and wiping furiously at his eyes.

"Who's that there?" he barked. Or coughed. It was difficult to tell. Especially muffled through the respirator.

Alice blinked through the mist, making her way toward him. "Um…my name is Alice." She kept her distance, always checking the darker pockets the light didn't reach. She eyed the exit across the way. "Just passing through. I -- "

"Alice, you say? Don't know an Alice. But no mind. Could you maybe give me hand here?" He lifted whatever he was working on into the air. "The rest are all above dumping our haul. I need to go help, but not until I get these stupid things fixed." He stopped, dropping his head and squeezing his eyes shut, again dabbing at them with his sleeve.

Alice wanted to move on, catch up to the boy, but the man looked rather pathetic, so she acquiesced and joined him near the pond.

"What's the problem?" she asked as she knelt nearby.

He held up what was in his lap, and Alice noticed his skin was oddly dry and scaly. "Damned eyepieces broke again." He glanced up at her, trying to focus through eyes that watered profusely.

"You ain't been down here before, have you?"

Alice shook her head. "No, why?"

The man pointed at her face. "Your eyes. If you spent any time down in these grottos, your eyes would be like mine -- damned metal dust. Now we all need these goggles down here to protect from the dust, and need 'em up there," he pointed to the hole in the rock above, "cuz we're too sensitive to the light."

Alice blinked again, beginning to feel the irritation of the particles in the air. "Then why stay down here?" she asked.

"Pfft...why do we what?" He squinted hard at her as though she might have an extra head or something. "Cuz if we don't gather the dust for *Her*, she'll put out head on a pike. Or, she won't give us our share. We do what we gotta."

He leaned toward her trying to focus. "How can you not know that?"

Flustered and not wanting any trouble, Alice tried to change the subject. "What's wrong with them?" She picked up the goggles.

"Rim lights went out. Need those to see down here because the glass is tinted for up there. But I can't bloody see to fix them!"

Alice settled on the ground and turned the goggles over. It didn't take her long to locate the wiring casing. It wasn't a major repair, but it was small -- just a tiny wire that had come loose from a connector. Easy to miss if your eyes were full of tears.

Pulling a multi-tool from her side pocket she quickly reattached the wire and checked the connection.

"Here you go." She handed the repaired goggles back to the man, who doused his eyes with water from a small container, and gave them one more wipe before slipping them on. Hitting a switch on the side, a ring of lights illuminated around the edges of the darkly tinted glass.

He looked at her then with clear eyes, scanning her up and down, noticing her pack, her weapon, her jacket, and pants. "Ah. Traveler, eh? Where from? You don't look like an Edger... The only one that ever comes in through here the way you did is the colorless one..." He gestures toward the exit where the boy had gone.

"Anyone else is either from the Outer Edge -- and they're all wild and stay out there -- or they are in the Settlements, which is the direction you're headed."

A gentle rumble vibrated over their heads and the man hunched and ducked just as a piece of stone fell loose and clanged off his back. That explained the back shield.

Alice flinched, moving clear, and her eyes were beginning to bother her. She wanted to move on. "Yeah, long story. And I really should push on. Can I help you with anything else?"

He patted her arm, smiling. "No, no. Fortuitous you came through, though. I hate sending the family up there without me."

Alice stood. "Okay then. Well..." She gestured to the doorway.

"Wait!" The man struggled to his feet on short, stubby legs that brought his head only to her chest, and waddled back the way she had come, disappearing into one of the rooms she had passed. When he returned, he handed her a small, woven basket in which she found dried meat, some berries, and a small loaf of bread.

She smiled and slipped the little basket into her pack. "Thank you."

"No -- thank you! I don't like not pulling my own weight, and making the family do too much of the work, so now I can help bring up our load so we can be done and take a much-needed break!"

He extended his hand, and Alice graciously shook it, then left him to his work, while she made her way to the other side of the grotto and back up into the world above.

The Maddening

Leaving the underground mole to his hole, Alice clambered up the incline on the other side and emerged back into the open air.

To her left, she could see a corrugated overhang near a concrete slab and a stretch of rail track. At the end of the track small carts sat in a line, and a group of people wearing tinted goggles emptied sacks into the bins on the carts. Old electrical poles lay in varied states of bent and broken, dead wires strewn and coiled nearby.

Behind them she saw a bevy of shacks. Some had makeshift porches, and there were clothes hanging on lines in the sunshine, children sitting on the ground stacking stones or playing with small, hand carved toys.

Straight ahead, up a rise that seemed to sweep its way around toward a river, stood a copse of trees.

Casting one, last glance over her shoulder to see the squat little man emerge from the hole and waddle over to the rail carts, the armor on his back making him look like a giant, metal turtle, she made her way up the hill.

On the other side of the hill, a handful of large, old houses emerged over the precipice, each with sweeping porches and gabled roofs, all in assorted stages of disarray and adorned with wild greenery pushing its way up through crevices and roofing and windows. She just caught sight of a handful of dogs trotting back behind the houses, noses to the ground. One looked strikingly familiar, but before she could confirm, they disappeared into the brush.

Beyond the houses, the hill became an outcrop of small boulders, beyond which lay a thicker stretch of woods.

The sun had again vanished behind dense, roiling clouds, the sky an odd shade of grayish green, the ever-present haze hanging dense and low.

Ahead she heard voices. Loud, raucous, although not angry, and with little concern over her direction -- other than forward -- she picked her way across the expanse of rock, avoiding large crevices and potholes, and climbed her way down toward the ground.

The space proved to be the most overgrown she'd come across, with snaking vines, and enormous trees -- some of which had snapped beneath their own weight, splitting in two and lying strewn across the ground.

A small rivulet of a stream trickled by on her left down a short, tumbling falls, along with toppled, broken statues; stone hands and cracked heads lay heaped in mud. She stopped a moment to look around at what she imagined had once been a park.

The sounds ahead caught her attention again, laughing mixing with the shouting, and something else...singing?

Down a small rise and around an old flower garden, with small, red buds on thorned branches trying desperately to become flowers again beneath a rather angry and unwelcoming sky, she saw them.

Three people, who appeared to be having a picnic -- a family? A blanket on the ground, bits of things scattered about, and a man, woman, and a girl perhaps a few years younger than herself alternately sitting or running around it, behaving like a very young child.

They were extremely active, maybe playing a game, or...maybe arguing...it was difficult to tell.

Behind them, slightly hidden by the overgrown trees, sat a small wooden structure -- simple, unassuming, made of stacked logs with open holes for windows and bark for roofing, Alice assumed it was their home. It was a stark difference to the ornate, stately once-homes she had just passed on the hill -- the ones that would have edged the park.

As she approached, she realized the woman had something on her head -- a hat? Although honestly, to Alice, it looked like her hair in a rather rats-nest fashion up all over her head. The woman constantly poked at it, slipping bits of debris from the ground into it as though arranging flowers.

She did not look well at all -- her face gaunt, her eyes wide, wild, unseeing, looking somewhere inward rather than out at the world. She chattered away to herself (since no one else seemed to be listening) occasionally clearly holding both sides of the conversation.

The girl, who did not look physically much healthier, skirted out across the blanket to grab something off a plate, then scampered back to a large, woven basket into which she climbed and snapped the cover shut, while the man -- her father? -- sat quietly, apparently oblivious to it all, rocking back and forth and twining a piece of string through his fingers.

They were an incredibly discomforting picture, and Alice thought it might be better to steer clear entirely.

Although she was admittedly curious.

The woman suddenly snapped her attention toward Alice, leaning forward, her head tipping back and forth. "We have guests!" She cried. "Is that today? I'm not ready!

"Or is it a surprise...I love surprises!" She clapped her hands together and jumped to her feet, spinning a quick circle before freezing in place.

"Except when I don't." Her face grew dark, accusatory, and she glared at Alice with disdain and mistrust. Alice backed away, jaw clenched, hand on her weapon. The hair on her neck raised, every muscle down her back tensed; this felt all wrong.

The girl reemerged from her basket, cradling something in her hand; it was the size of her fist, rounded, metallic. "Humpty Dumpty sat on a wall," the little girl sang as she set the item down, balanced on the edge of the basket.

It was a grenade.

Shit.

Alice tensed, looking around for cover.

"Humpty-Dumpty had a great fall..." Alice froze in place, holding her breath, unable to will herself to move as the girl tapped the grenade and in slow, time-warped motion, it tumbled, end-over-end, a straight-forward plunge -- and hit the ground with a thud.

Alice clenched her eyes shut, breathless.

Nothing.

She huffed in relief and swallowed the lump in her throat. Slowly she opened her eyes and took a full, steadying breath.

The girl looked up at Alice while remaining close to her basket. "Have you come for brunch?" Mommy -- they are here for brunch."

Alice looked around to see who "they" might be, but she was alone.

"That doesn't look like brunch." The father turned, eyeing her with an empty, desolate, slightly predatory gaze.

Alice put up her hands. "Yeah...um...no. I'm good. Just passing through -- "

"I DON'T LIKE SURPRISES!" The woman screamed out, snatching and pulling at her hair-hat.

Alice flinched, "What the fuck!?"

The woman railed on, "And I'm not dressed for company! This is not my formal hat! Why are people such barbarians?!"

She seemed distressed that she could not remove her hair, becoming increasingly agitated each time she tried.

"NO TIME FOR BRUNCH!" The man roared. "They'll be here to collect soon, and I don't see anything here for them to take!" He looked wildly about the space, although he didn't move from his spot, and Alice heard him whimper -- a pitiful, sorrowful sound.

At the sound of him yelling, the girl ducked inside the basket, out of sight, and Alice stood, bewildered and uneasy.

Suddenly Chester's face swam into view a few feet behind the woman. He wore a tinted face mask, his gaze actively scanning the ground.

Alice paused to watch as the rest of him slowly materialized.

Chester waved for her to stop. "I wouldn't go any closer if I were you."

Alice froze, looking around. "Why?"

"You're in The Maddening," he said, gesturing around them, and down to the party on the blanket.

"The *Maddening*?" she asked, not sure she cared for an explanation.

"Yep. Here..." Stooping to retrieve a stone, he tossed it to a space a between herself and the blanket. When it hit the ground it struck something that caused a spark, a pop, and the rock exploded into dust.

"What the hell is that?"

"Keeps them right where they are," Chester answered, pointing to the strange family. "And keeps others away."

"But why?" Alice asked, in spite of not truly wanting to know.

"Remember you asked me why people don't try and get through the Breach?" Chester paced as he spoke, carefully wandering back and forth in front of the crazy picnic people, his eyes behind the mask focused on the ground, choosing his steps with caution and precision.

Alice just nodded, unable to look away from the grim, creepy scene before her, the girl peeking out from inside her hideout to throw a piece of trash which hit another spot on the ground and blew into bits.

She looked around her feet and stood extremely still.

Chester paused. "Well, these folks are here as an example of what will happen if anyone tries. And if they move from their spot, the ground is littered with little landmines -- some explosive, some rigged like -- well -- like the marbles I gave you but with some seriously gruesome things. Might not kill you, but it'll leave you pretty -- damaged.

"Earned this place the name The Maddening."

"What happened to *them*?" Alice looked away as the father turned toward her, seeming to stare directly through her. Like he could see what she was thinking.

"Crimsa happened to them. Don't ask me what. I don't need to know. But they got caught, and rather than their head on a pike, she did something worse to them and sent them back like this."

"Jesus..." Alice breathed.

Chester held up his finger and trained his gaze on the ground, picking his way over and around the space until he reached her. Then he guided her through the danger zone and onto safe ground.

Once clear, he lifted his mask with a grin. "This lets me see the grid, so I know where they are."

"So I guess I'm rather lucky..."

"Yup. Although you were only a few steps in. But I think if you'd moved just half a step to your right..."

The father was agitated, up on his feet, glaring at Alice.

She instinctively backed away, grasping her gun, even though she didn't think he'd make a move.

Without warning and with a screeching howl, he lunged forward, "I won't let you take them!" he screamed, making it three or four steps before landing on an explosive that went off in a blinding flash.

He screeched and fell to the ground, grasping his leg, his foot mangled and nearly blown off.

At the same time, the image of a horrific, horned beast appeared; half decayed, dripping slime, it rose overhead on leathery wings, dive-bombing the girl and her mother with deafening roars.

Alice knew it wasn't real -- although contact could do damage -- but even she felt terror watching it swirl through the air. She could only imagine how it appeared to a broken, fragile mind.

The mother dropped to the ground, cowering in fear, while the little girl's shrill laughter spun up into the overcast sky as she twirled around in a sickening dance. That's when Alice realized the child was missing half her right arm. The mother just pulled bits of her tangled hair down over her ears and clamped her eyes shut as the man's agonizing cries died down to a numbing whimper. He haphazardly wrapped a ragged napkin around his blasted leg as the projected beast finally blew apart in an explosion of smoke.

Alice turned away. She'd seen enough. And there was nothing she could do.

A deep thrum rose from nowhere and vibrated through the air. Alice could feel it in her breastbone.

Lifting her gaze, she saw a pulsing glow far in the distance. She could see faint structures rising through the haze, but only barely as the smolder bled out into the surrounding sky.

The sound seemed to emanate from there.

Chester also followed the sound with his gaze. "Water processing is finished. She'll be dolling it out over the next few days."

Alice glanced at him out of the corner of her eye, but only briefly. The sound beyond held her attention.

"*She?*" Alice turned to ask Chester, but he was gone.

She couldn't help but look back once more to the pathetic, crazed family -- the father had dragged himself back to the blanket where the girl skittered over to help tend his wound. The mother slowly pulled the blanket off the ground, dumping everything off it in the process, and buried herself beneath it.

Alice wondered what they were like before. Where did they live? Why did they risk leaving? They were sad, and frightening, and -- maddening, yes. Not just mad/crazy, but mad/angry. Crimsa's rules were horrifically cruel.

Leaving them, she started across the park, keeping one eye on the heavy sky, which looked like it might be gearing up for another downpour. She found an opening through some brambles and climbed through it into the overgrowth.

The foliage quickly grew dark and dense, the air itself damp, dank, and oppressive.

Pulling out her weapon, she used the axe to cut through thick vines and brush, climbing over fallen trees and under branches, while keeping eyes and ears tuned toward what might lie beyond her view.

Without a sound, an enormous white bird startled her as it swooped just overhead, crossing her path and diving down near a tangle of bushes on the other side. Alice froze as a scuffle ensued out of sight, and after a moment, the bird emerged again, a large rabbit in its long, sharp claws, and it lit on a tree branch a few yards away.

Alice remained still, holding her breath.

It stared down at her as though daring her to take its prize -- wide, round, unblinking eyes focused and unmoving.

That's when she noticed it.

Hidden within the leaves, a small, black, glass orb reflecting dappled light, and emitting a barely-perceptible hum.

As she stepped forward, the bird snatched up its prey and took to higher branches.

The glass eye hummed and hissed, the aperture whining closed, then open, spinning on its axis to follow her.

She was being watched.

But by whom? And if they knew she was there, why didn't they come get her?

Strolling around the other side of the tree, she found a lower branch on which to boost herself up. From there it was easy to climb to where the camera perched, and she came up behind it; small, cobbled together with odd bits of metal and machinery, a thin wire snaked up the trunk of the tree toward the top.

Alice wondered if there was a network of wires up there, all connecting together and leading toward one power source.

If so, she was pretty sure she knew where that would be.

After yanking the wire out of the back of the unit, she reversed her path and dropped back to the ground.

The afternoon had grown late, the light in the woods less, and she wanted to be out of there before dark. Dark in the middle of woods was a different kind of dark.

A little farther on she stumbled on a faint path - - foliage and ground cover slightly stamped down and cut back. She followed it a bit, hoping it would lead her out.

But after a short walk, she came across a small, stone structure, a steel tower beside it rising up toward the treetops, cables running from the structure to the tower and vanishing in the trees. A buzz came from the stone shack.

Power.

Huh. She thought, considering the electric eye she had passed earlier.

The door to the building unexpectedly swung open and a tall, absurdly lanky man ducked through the opening and onto the path in front of her.

He startled when he finally pulled himself up straight. "Oh! What? Who -- " he fumbled over his own words, clearly not accustomed to coming across anyone.

A ruddy scarf kept stringy hair out of his eyes and a pocketed belt around his waist held an assortment of tools. His face was long, thin, his nose nearly a beak in the middle of it all. On his feet he wore large, wide, boots wrapped and patched with cloth and tape which, to Alice, made him look like he had enormous paws for feet.

He and Alice did a momentary dance on the path, each trying to pass the other.

"I'm sorry…" Alice mumbled as she tried to go to the right.

"Why?" The wiry man twitched and lurched as he spoke. "Did you do something?"

Alice stood still, confused a moment. "Uh…no…I mean, just trying to get out of your way. Don't want to bother you…"

He peered at her, clacking his teeth together and fiddling with the tools on his belt. "Ah. Is that all? I thought maybe you were the one who cut the feed on the BugEye."

Alice froze, afraid maybe he had seen her in the tree and was looking to apprehend her.

"BugEye?" she asked.

The man stumbled, stuttered, rethinking having said anything. "Er…nothing…nothing…I just need to go fix it…"

He dropped his gaze to the ground and shifted his feet to step around her. He stopped again. "You didn't see anyone else around here did you?"

Alice shook her head. "No. Sorry… Um…shouldn't the -- BugEye -- show you who damaged it?" She chanced asking to find out if she'd been seen.

The man's snake-like arm waved her away. "Pfft. Stupid things can barely see. But I gotta keep 'em working anyway, just in case -- "

He caught himself again, saying more than he ought. Clearly, no one was supposed to know about the BugEyes.

"Never mind." He became irritated, short. "Stop bothering me! I have a job to do! Please, step out of my way."

Alice stepped aside and gestured for him to continue on his way.

After watching him disappear into the brush, she looked around in the trees overhead, checked her compass, and continued through the woods. She needed higher or clearer ground, and she needed the boy in white.

She needed to get home.

Wickets

Alice had a difficult time making heads or tails of where she was. The landscape seemed to shift on a whim, and she couldn't tell if she was on the edges of a city, the remnants of a town, or just jumbled mix of places made incomprehensible by time, damage, and a fair amount of abuse and neglect.

People really fucked up this world, she thought. She could imagine what the places she'd been through had been like once. She wished she could have seen it.

But, while the Downer was not anything like what she'd been told, it was still all crap now. Every bit of it.

And she had completely lost track of the boy.

The tangle of woods eventually began to thin and open up. While it never completely vanished, it did give way to larger buildings several stories tall. Some of them spanned a few blocks. Alice had never seen buildings so large or built so densely -- although much of them were obscured by overgrown trees and other foliage. The trees, like the buildings, fell in varying states of decay and disarray, forcing her to climb over and under toppled trunks as well as cars, bins and general debris.

Looking up, she saw where strong, thick trunks had pushed their way through foundations and floors, reaching up and out of windows. Sometimes it was hard to tell if the tree grew through the building, or the building had been built around the tree. Although she knew which one it was. Nature wanted its world back, turning it into a concrete and glass forest.

As enclosed and desolate as the streets were, here, too, she could feel the life that had once filled this space. While long since gone, the sense of them echoed -- it was eerie.

All of these windows once held people, homes, shops. And there were so *many*.

It was hard to picture so much -- life.

A whistle cut through the air overhead and Alice whirled, looking up toward the windows behind her just in time to see a head vanish from view.

Across the street, the sound of a tumble of trash -- cans and bottles falling to the pavement clattered and echoed.

Another whistle behind and to her left.

Alice walked forward, not slowing or showing any sign of concern, but she tuned in on the sounds around her: a shuffle in an alley beyond some boxes. A bark up ahead answered by one around a corner. A sharp whistle, this one trilling up before ending with a door slam.

Her stomach tightened and she realized she disliked the overgrown, overbuilt enclosed streets more than the open fields. Things could be anywhere around her and she wouldn't see them until they were on top of her.

Passing an alley slightly blocked by a dumpster, she quickly scanned the shadows within it and dove against the brick wall behind the bin.

Her breath grew short and sharp, and she wiped the sweat from her forehead. Bruises there made her wince.

For the first time since she'd gotten to The Downer she felt truly afraid. Like, this-is-not-good, I'm-on-my-own-in-unfamiliar-terrain-and-one-shitty-shotgun kind of scared. If she was attacked here by whatever was whistling and banging and making a racket, she wasn't sure she'd make it out alive.

Now would be a good time for Chester.

For a moment it went quiet, but then she heard boots on pavement and the raucous chatter of voices. Peering around the dumpster she could just make out an enormous storefront through a gap between the overgrowth. It was a bit farther down the street than she had gotten so she hadn't noticed it. But now she could see a few people gathering, crossing the street toward it.

Inching her way closer to the mouth of the alley, she noticed that most seemed older than her, though there were a few near her age. And there were more than a few. A dozen or two, easily, and while clad in different degrees of dirt and scruff, some with long-handled mallets slung over their shoulders, they seemed at ease with one another...

"Hey...are you coming?" A voice to her left startled her and Alice leapt to her feet, grabbing at her shotgun.

"What?" It came out of her before she registered who had asked.

"To Wickets. You coming? It's the last night before they shut down again for a month to brew and dry."

Alice took in the speaker. A guy slightly older than herself, an oversized black jacket with heavy, rusty clasps over his lanky frame, his trousers frayed at the knee and tucked into heavy, knee-high boots. A belt at his waist held a small pistol and a knife, but his face, half hidden behind a mop of hair as dark as his jacket, smiled.

"Brew and dry?" was all Alice could muster, the thrumming of her heart stealing her breath. Her hand gripped the butt of her rifle.

The young man squinted at her and looked her up and down. "You're new here, aren't you? Wickets opens for a few days once a month. It takes that long to make milk mead -- at least the good kind. And it takes a little less than that to dry the Kaveria leaves..."

Alice hadn't realize it, but she had begun walking with him as he talked. When he mentioned the leaves, the name struck a familiar chord and she stopped.

"Kaveria...like tea?"

The guy smiled. "Sure. If you drink it..."

They had walked the block down to the place he referred to as "Wickets". She looked up to see the building scaled at least a dozen floors, but the bottom was an enormous atrium currently full of people.

Over the doorway hung a metal slab painted with a large arch wound with spiny red roses.

Alice hesitated and glanced around, taking a few steps away. "Yeah, you know what? Thanks for the invite, but..."

"C'mon. Get something to eat at least. You look like you haven't eaten in a while. At least not much."

At the mention of food, Alice caught the scent of a fire and something roasting. Her mouth flooded with saliva. She wanted to keep going, to find the boy, to get home. She was also starving, tired, and the sun was beginning to set.

While she did not relish the idea of a building full of people she didn't know, she also knew that crowds meant places for someone small, strong and lithe, to vanish quickly. And actual food would renew her strength.

Warily and alert, she followed her host in.

Immediately Alice was hit by a wall of heat -- people, smoke, the aroma of cooking meat, the pungent scent of things smoked or sipped assaulted her, fogging her focus.

She shook it off quickly though and scanned her surroundings. While the entrance was a large, open hall, it was also densely packed. Makeshift tables and crate chairs lined the perimeter. In the center, an enormous spit roasted something big and unidentifiable. A counter wrapped around that, lined with people milling around drinking something cloudy out of jars and mismatched cups, while other appeared to be playing various games around larger tables. Men and women, their faces painted in swirls of red that reminded Alice of the flowers trying to bloom near the Maddening made their way around the room doling out jars of drink.

"I'm Aaron, by the way," her host leaned in to say in her ear as he led her to a table in the corner. She was glad to see it was near the front door, and she took a moment to notice other options: a set of windows across the way, glass gone, only one boarded up, and a doorway around the counter and past the spit.

"Alice," she breathed as she set down in a chair with easy access to escape.

She looked around the room, taking in a completely unfamiliar sight: people relaxed, happy, laughing.

While Aaron went to get something to eat and drink, two women across the room erupted briefly, exchanging a few punches before someone came up with two jars of milky drink and broke them up. But that was the only disruption she saw. Even those playing what appeared to be a game with sets of cards strewn across the table between them, hands flying from stacks to piles, slapping down loudly with a holler when they won, even there, the loser did so happily, ready to deal and play again.

Alice looked up as Aaron returned with a plate of whatever charred on the spit, and two jars of the strange, cloudy drink. She sniffed it and wrinkled her nose; it smelled spicy, sweet and just a tad acrid.

Aaron smiled, "Milk mead!"

He raised his jar, and while Alice was hesitant to trust anyone, she desperately wanted to relax -- even if for a minute. She studied his face, his skin pale, his eyes a cavernous, muddy brown and deeply inhaled the smell of the meat on her plate. "Oh what the hell," she acquiesced, and clinked her glass to his.

She took a sip and pursed her lips, "Ehm...woah..."

"Sweet with a kick!" Aaron grinned as he took a gulp that emptied half the glass.

Alice now understood why everyone was so happy.

She picked a hunk of meat off her plate and ate it. It was warm, sweet, and so much better than the dry bread, meats and nuts she had in her pack. Her eyes closed as she let the flavors sink in.

"I was right that you haven't eaten well in a while, wasn't I?" Aaron asked.

Alice was about to answer, her mouth full of the rich, savory meat, when an air horn blast erupted from somewhere beyond the back of the building. Nearly everyone left their table games, plates and empty glasses, chairs scraping back against the floor en masse as they all pushed around the center counter and toward the rear of the building. A few pockets of people remained, seemingly content to miss the whatever they were being called to.

Aaron's face lit up as he, too, rose from his seat. "Game time!"

Alice remained seated, confused. "Game time?"

"Tournament day for the Pike games!" Aaron casually explained. "C'mon..." He held out his hand for her to follow.

Biting her lip and glancing around, Alice considered declining and moving on, grabbing a handful of bread and meat from her plate. But Aaron was already seizing her arm and pulling her up out of her seat, down the side hallway beyond the roasting meat and out a back door.

Outside, Alice stopped. A large, overgrown courtyard between towering buildings had been cleared out, revealing a stone and dirt plaza surrounded by creeping vines and ancient, invading, gnarly trees. The denizens of Wickets sat around the perimeter on edges of stone walls and makeshift tables and chairs, while two handfuls of players took to opposite sides of the plaza, swinging mallets playfully through the air. In the center of the field in a chalk circle, sat a disturbingly realistic looking, although grossly mangled, severed head.

"This used to be battle play," Aaron explained as the two took a seat at a small table a short way into the courtyard. Alice continued to enjoy her meal as she listend to Aaron.

"Crimsa's terror cry of "Heads will Roll" inspired a training game for the rebels." He pointed to the center of the open space, "Crimsa's head as a ball, with two factions trying to seize control of it and plant it on their pike at the end of the field. The head can only be passed by rolling it on the ground or whacking it with a mallet, and you took out other players by, well, it *was* battle training…it was pretty brutal."

Alice raised her eyebrows and glanced from Aaron to the players in the courtyard. "You said 'was' battle training. Isn't it anymore?"

Aaron shook his head. "In spirit, but not really. Now you take opponents out by tripping them up with the handle of the mallet. Knock them off their feet. They have to stay down for five seconds. It's really just to blow off steam. Have fun. You know, fun, right?"

A simple question, but Alice couldn't answer him right away. She tried to remember. But then another thought struck. "Wait -- this is pretty ballsy. I mean, doesn't Crimsa provide all this?" She gestured around her, to Wickets behind them full of spicy meats and sweet drinks. "Doesn't everyone somehow work for her here? I thought that's how it worked."

Aaron bristled and then laughed. "Crimsa? Are you kidding? She has no idea we are out here."

Alice stopped. "What?"

"If she knew we had all this here...yeah, I don't think so."

With every turn The Downer proved not what she thought. "What about guard patrols?"

"What about them?" Aaron drained his glass and set it on the ground nearby. On the field, a horn blew and the head was snatched from the chalk circle as the small crowd cheered for their chosen team.

"Well...I mean..."

Aaron waved her off. Then he leaned in close, gesturing for her to do the same. "Honestly, I don't think Crimsa's what she used to be. Or her guards. Haven't seen them around for...gee..." He stood back again, gazing across the plaza before returning to her. "For as long as I can remember."

Alice stared at him, taking it in, trying to piece together the truth of The Downer. She also realized she needed to get moving. She needed to find the boy, get the key, get back home to Lily before...

Lily...

From nowhere, a tall woman with long, copper hair in a single braid over her shoulder appeared at Aaron's side and laid a hand on him. Her bare forearms were thick, sinewy, her upper arms each wrapped in leather strapping. She was clearly a fighter.

"Hey Aaron, why don't you stop talking now?"

Aaron rolled his eyes and put up his hand to wave her away, but she grabbed it, pulling him out of his chair and taking his place.

"Jesus, Duchess -- paranoid much?" He snarled.

Duchess stared at Alice, her eyes narrowing. Alice pushed slightly away from the table, her gaze flicking toward Aaron nearby.

"We don't get many wanderer's around here, " she scowled, one arm leaning on the table, the other clearly perched on the butt of her blade. "Especially not alone. No one travels alone unless...unless they know they are safe. Protected..."

Alice's gaze flicked from the woman across from her, to Aaron -- who watched warily.

"I don't know what you are talking about... who -- "

The woman kicked out her chair and jumped to her feet, towering over Alice. "Don't play with us, " she spit. "Crimsa would love to get her hands on us and what we've made here -- "

"You think I'm from Crimsa's?" Alice stood, spinning her chair between herself and the woman. "Do I *look* like a guard?" She gestured to her clothing.

"No, but as you've just heard, we know the guards aren't what they used to be. Maybe she's recruiting spies..." Duchess stepped toward Alice.

Aaron grabbed her by the arm, "Duchess, let her be. I don't think -- "

But Duchess wrenched free, knocking Aaron down and whipping back toward Alice.

Alice didn't wait for more banter or to see how this would play out. Instead, she whipped her shotgun-axe around her shoulder as she planted her foot against the chair and shoved it hard toward Duchess.

The game came to an abrupt halt. Stumbling backward, Duchess grabbed for the knife on her belt as two others flanked her: a young guy, his head shaved, revealing multiple scars, and wearing layers of overlapping shirts, and a smaller woman, stocky and low to the ground, her hair a mop of curls held out of her eyes in a wrapped scarf. Everyone else simply paused to take note, but remained where they were, content to watch it unfold without getting involved.

Alice scanned the plaza but couldn't make out a clear exit path. She quickly grabbed the edge of the makeshift table, flipping it up and sending the drinks flying toward all of them as she fired a single shot in the direction of the guy behind Duchess.

She grazed him, but not badly.

Alice then spun toward the back door of the building but was met by the short, stocky woman who swung a mallet in a sweeping arc toward her head.

It narrowly missed Alice who ducked, swinging her own weapon, axe first, connecting with the woman's leg, nearly severing it at the knee.

As the woman went down with a deep, bellowing howl, Alice rolled to the right, leaping again to her feet, and careened back through the door into the building.

She could hear Duchess right behind her, and Aaron calling after as she slid around the roasting spit.

Duchess fired a shot that caught the edge of Alice's shoulder. She stumbled. People scattered as she ducked behind them, between tables, around the counter, leaping up again, spinning half way around and firing her shotgun, catching Duchess square in the chest.

She didn't stay to watch her fall.

Instead Alice turned, plowing through the remaining group of people and out the open window across the atrium.

"Alice, wait!" She heard Aaron, but she didn't stop.

She tumbled onto a crate, stumbled over a pile of trash, scattering a group of unnervingly large rats, and ran through the twilight until her breath came dry and rasping.

Looking up, she found herself in front of a brownstone. Tripping up the stairs she kicked open the front door, turned right into the first room she saw and stumbled back to a far corner near what had been the bathroom.

There she sank down, breath heaving, hand tight on her bloody shoulder, and coughed out the dust in her lungs.

"Fucking shit," she breathed into the growing darkness, thankful that no one had followed her.

No. She thought, finally. *I do **not** know fun.*

The Bay

After digging out a rag and using some of her water to clean out the wound, Alice wrapped her shoulder and collapsed against the back wall. It didn't help. She was injured. For real.

The moon rose full, struggling to shine through the murky clouds, casting a dim, muddy hue into the building.

Her eyes burned and she pressed the heels of her hands hard into them, fighting the tears that threatened to spill..

She was tired. Afraid. She wanted to get home. Lily needed her.

Lily

"Aaaahhhh! Sonofabitch!" she screamed into the darkness, hurling a chunk of broken plaster into the shadows, angry at the tears. Angry at her pain. Angry.

A scuffle near the door brought her shotgun up, but she realized she hadn't reloaded. She grit her teeth. "Who the fuck is there? I swear to god, I'll -- "

She didn't finish because Chester slowly came into view, his hands raised in front of him. He crept toward her, kneeling when he got close.

Alice dropped her gun and exhaled. "Godammit, Chester. Seriously. One of these times you're gonna get shot." She flipped her bag off her shoulder and dug in a pocket for shells and reloaded the gun.

"You're hurt." Chester reached for her shoulder.

She shrugged him away. "I'm fine."

She caught his eye. "Are you following me?" she asked him.

Chester just grinned at her, and pulled a small pack from the back of his belt. Opening it, he took out small jars and wads of fabric, and set out tending to her wound.

"You're lucky. It just grazed you."

She flinched as he cut away a bit of her sleeve to get to the wound. "Yeah, well...still hurts like hell, so I'd appreciate it if you took it easy."

Chester cleaned the wound and took a closer look. "Yeah, you're gonna need a few stitches…"

Alice clenched her jaw, hot, angry, exhausted tears burning behind her eyes. "Whatever," she bit the words off. "Just do it."

Once he had cleaned it a bit more, Alice dug her fingers into the side of her leg and took short, quick breaths as he began stitching the wound closed. He was quick, adept, distracting Alice with chatter she paid no attention to, making her think he had done this before. When finished, he applied some kind of salve, bandaged it, and sat back, squatting a short distance away from her. It had grown dark, and she could barely make out his silhouette.

Through tight, pursed lips, Alice released a long stream of air from her lungs, and tried to ignore both the dull throb in her shoulder and push of exhausted tears. Pulling out her flashlight, she checked the power remaining and clicked it on, standing it up on the floor. It cast an uneven wedge of light between them.

"You'll be safe here tonight," Chester said. "If you head out tomorrow and go northwest, you'll find a street that opens up and leads up a small incline toward the river. Head that way to find the boy."

Alice massaged her neck and tried to ignore the pain in her shoulder, which was almost impossible.

She closed her eyes, fighting the part of her that wanted to punch Chester for fading in and out of existence like this. Appearing and leaving with no forewarning, helping, but only kind of.

She decided to tell him that, but when she opened her eyes he was gone. Only the small medical bag was left on the floor where he'd been.

The morning broke hazy and thin, as usual. Alice realized she'd actually slept for the first time in days, and woke truly rested. After taking a few bites of the food the turtle/mole man had given her, she gently rolled her shoulder and lifted her arm to test the pain. Whatever Chester had used had dulled the sharpness, leaving it feeling just bruised and sore. Nevertheless, she stayed mindful of the stitches as she slipped her gun onto her back, picked up her pack, and headed for the door.

Peaking around the opening she checked the streets. It was quiet. Empty. Taking a look at her compass to get her bearings, she headed in the direction Chester told her.

Sure enough, she crossed an empty lot and into a field with a line of trees on a long, large berm that reached the river. On the other side, a wide, open avenue.

She could cut straight across, or she could arc her way around along the tree line.

While it would take longer, she opted for the hill and the trees, which would provide some options for protective cover.

Looking around, out over the open expanse, she didn't see anything that appeared to be small, white, and running. She heaved a full, exhausted sigh. She was tired of chasing him. She was also afraid she had lost the boy's trail altogether.

What then?

The ground was all short scrub brush, some dried and brittle, some a kind of evergreen, stubbornly reaching out into surrounding areas, all of it stiff and rough. Scanning the vista, she again tried to imagine it as the stories described it, tried to see everything deep green, littered with colorful wildflowers, dark, fertile earth.

She glanced behind her at the wildly reclaimed high rises and blocks of concrete wound through with greenery.

How much wanton, selfishness did it take to leave it stripped so barren, so completely opposite of what it once was? How did anyone let it get that far?

Living as she did with her sister -- as they *all* lived: making what they could, finding what they had to, bartering whenever possible, and always, it seemed, on the verge of annihilation, she never thought much about it. Always existing on the brink of finally, utterly running out of everything, and yet somehow always managing to discover something to grow, a new way to build and so, a way forward -- it was just how things were.

But now, standing there, overlooking a huge expanse of what had once been lush, dense, healthy -- she could not imagine a life where you never had to wonder where the food, water, power, air would come from. It just was -- there. Waiting.

How could anyone let *that* become *this*?

Hiking through a stand of trees, where she thought she'd meet the river on the other side, she instead came upon a small bay, adorned with a handful of rusted out, broken down hulls. Empty specters of a once-thriving port.

Ducking beneath branches, and pulling brambles off her pants, she stepped out onto the rocky shore.

She'd never seen so much water -- although it lay still, and murky, a green and copper tinge swirling around on its surface. it was, nevertheless, water. More than she'd ever laid eyes on, all the way to the horizon in one direction. The empty deserted hulls, half tipped over or upended -- while ghostly, and strange, and ominous -- were also rather beautiful in a haunting, reminiscent way. Everything contained a kind of aura of what used to be.

She stood awhile, gazing out across the small inlet toward nearly flattened wooden structures and docks on the other side, everything listing as though exhausted and having exhaled their final breath.

In front of the buildings, she caught sight of the boy, his small figure moving around within a small gaggle of others. There appeared to be a little gathering of animals as well, milling about in and around the broken down structures at the shore.

Alice ducked back into the tree line and ran for the docks, leaping logs and tangles of vines while keeping one eye on the boy in white.

When she came near, she slowed, moving around toward the back, edging along the base of a hill that ran behind the buildings. She climbed up onto a concrete slab on which the buildings sat and used the old crates and truck containers to slip around and behind.

She was able to get close enough to see a large opening in one of the buildings. Inside, she could just make out a couple adults, a few children, and a smattering of animals -- small foul and horned goats.

Alice slid along the wall of the building careful to keep her pack and her gun from scraping or banging against it until she was near the door. Then she crouched behind a pile of broken crates and listened, peeking through gaps between the boards of the building.

The boy in white knelt down in a slant of sun, the air full of dust, and patted the head of a small dog while a woman holding a young child stood nearby. They spoke quietly at first, the boy chattering fast, his face animated and worried.

The woman stood, her ashen hair falling just to her shoulders in scrunched, bunched waves that the toddler pulled her fingers through.

The boy glanced up to her, his voice small and quiet, but then he turned and the sound carried out to Alice. "The guards won't bother you anymore. There aren't enough of them left, really." He slipped the dog a treat.

Alice noticed other animals now, out across the concrete, in an enclosure near the water: two goats, and three chickens that she could see. She also realized that the plants growing up closer to the building were purposeful -- a garden.

That's when she also noticed the other sounds -- like pumps and machinery, metal clanking. Peering through the slats into the darkness at the back of the building, she saw a man and a boy manually pumping a see-saw mechanism. She could hear gentle pulses and suction and assumed they were filtering water from the bay.

The boy then removed his weapon and set it on a table nearby along with a pouch of ammunition.

"Just in case, " he said to the woman. "It's not a lot, but I'll try and get more for it later."

The woman's eyes filled with tears and she knelt down to him. Now that Alice had gotten a decent look, she thought he must be around ten or eleven years old. She also noticed something around his neck…like a collar with a small panel of blinking, red lights. The boy slipped a finger along the edge and rubbed beneath it.

"Oh, Bolain…" the woman sighed. "You have been so brave through this, my boy." Her breath caught, and she stopped, fighting tears. "I miss you. I wish we could get you home."

Alice held her breath. The sounds behind them ebbed away and the others stepped out of the shadows; a young boy, an older girl, and a man. When he stepped into the light Alice saw he was nearly as pale as the boy. His light hair curly and long, he wore a shabby shirt -- patched and repaired with the sleeves rolled up -- his pants heavy and thick, but worn.

He put his arm around the woman and laid a hand on the shoulder the boy they called Bolain, and then pulled him close in a hug. "She's right...you've been brave. But we all miss you."

Bolain looked up to them both and they came together in what Alice realized was a familial embrace. This was his family!

His father pulled away and examined the rifle. "Bolain -- if there are as few as you say -- why don't you just leave? Come home. If they come, we will deal with it. Maybe we can finally end this."

Bolain hesitated. He clearly wanted to agree, but wasn't able.

Alice had been crouching so long, her legs stiff and tight, that she suddenly lost her balance, her boot scuffing along the concrete and her arm grabbing onto the pile of crates.

The sound startled all of them and without a thought, without pause, Bolain took off like a shot, out a crack in the wall that led to the docks.

The father snatched the gun from the table. "Who's there!" he demanded.

Alice took a deep breath and slowly, her hands in the air in a show of non-aggression, she stood and stepped into the opening.

"I'm so sorry," she said, unmoving, making it clear she wasn't a threat.

The mother and other children retreated back into the shadows as the father stepped forward, gun lowered. "I'll ask you again -- who are you?"

Alice faltered a moment. "My name is Alice. I've been trying to catch up to -- your son?"

No one acknowledged her so she continued. "I'm from the other side of the Breach. I fell through when your son opened a door and I've been trying to catch up to him to ask him to help me get back..."

The man eyed her, looking her over, trying to determine is she was telling the truth.

He relaxed his hold on the gun a little. "You definitely don't look like you are from Crimsa's guard."

"What? No!" Alice exclaimed, pointing to her various bruises and scrapes. "See these? Courtesy of the men in metal. I'm not from here, I promise. But -- if I may...why did he run?"

The man looked over his shoulder toward the hole in the wall where his son had scrambled away.

"He thought they had sent you. To find him."

"Why? If -- if you don't mind. Why isn't he here with you?" Alice risked dropping her arms and relaxing just a bit.

The woman stepped forward again, her children staying behind, each peering around her at Alice. "That would be because of me. I fell ill after

Illya's birth." She gestured to the toddler. "We were caught trying to take medicinals -- more than our allotment. We could have been killed, but Crimsa offered banishment to the fields to survive on our own if we handed over Bolain to be her servant. He's good with machinery and small -- " She stopped, her words choked in her throat.

Alice waved her hand. "I understand. Please. You don't have to say anymore. I'm so sorry." She ventured further into the building.

"I'm also sorry I frightened him. I didn't mean for that to happen. Can I ask...what was he doing outside the Breach?"

The two exchanged a quick glance, clearly uncertain anything more should be said.

Alice tried to reassure them. "I swear, I'm not from here. I'm not from Crimsa's. How would I know he'd been outside the Breach unless I saw him there? Unless I had come from there myself?"

The man shifted his weight and relaxed his shoulders. "He was looking for weapons and ammunition for us," his father answered. "Crimsa demanded Bolain because he's good with his hands. He hacked the Breach to get out beyond and see what he could find that we didn't have here...for us. For his mother. He cannot take from Crimsa -- she would know. So he began sneaking out to forage around.

Alice sighed and closed her eyes. "Shit. I'm so sorry. I -- I can't imagine." She looked at this family and thought of her own, imagined being torn apart.

For a moment the world wavered, Alice growing woozy, something gnawing at the back of her mind. She needed to get home.

While his mother remained back in the shadows, clearly upset by the whole encounter, Bolain's father grew bolder. "And may I ask *you* why you came through into The Downer? If it did, indeed, happen as you say."

"I was being chased. I got caught between my attackers and the Breach, and Bolain just happened to be there opening a passage. I didn't have much choice, so I jumped after him."

She imagined how she'd feel if it was Lily who was taken from her, wincing as she fought of an unexpected retching in her stomach. Was she ill? Was her wound infected?

"If I find him, " Alice asked, trying to quell the dizziness, "can he help me get back home, back through the Breach?"

Again the parents exchanged a look. The mother turned and walked away while the father lowered his gaze. "I don't know. I mean, he's capable, but whether he'll be able to depends on where he is when you reach him. *If* you reach him."

Alice looked behind her out the door. She needed to get going. "How long does he have to stay with Crimsa?"

The boy's father met her gaze. "Until she says so."

Alice's heart ached. Then she raged. There was no reason for any of this. Clearly there is plenty here. If there is water, and animals, there must be more caves like the grotto with metal dust for fuel cells. None of them should have to live like this.

"If I can find him, maybe I can help. Maybe we can get you all through with me." She had no idea how she might make that happen, but she couldn't look at this family, couldn't imagine Bolain running through this wasteland alone back to his prison, and not offer *something*.

The man just smiled but shook his head. "Thank you, but -- don't make impossible promises. We've learned to accept things.

"You should go."

Alice looked from one to the other, wishing there was more she could do, but simply nodded, and turned toward the door.

Down by the River

The sun lifted higher in the sky, struggling to cast its frail, ineffectual light.

Without a word, Alice slipped out past the garden and the animals and jumped down onto the rocky shore. She made her way back past the rusted out, decaying hulls and into the shadows of the trees.

Closer to the river she found what looked like an old shantytown. Ramshackle structures like the ones on the outskirts of where she lived that went up shortly after The Fall, built by tribes of people who had taken to a quasi-nomadic life.

All the buildings seemed empty now, though. Alice couldn't shake a strange, odd feeling -- the sense of those who had once lived here. Like all of The Downer, there seemed a vestigial sense of the life that had once infused the place. If filled the air like a thing, itself -- a constant, nagging reminder of all those that had been before.

She could almost see them moving about, talking, laughing, cooking; she could imagine families -- whole, together, happy.

The Downer was a far more desolate -- although dense -- place than she had imagined. But it hadn't always been that way. The longer she traveled, the more evident that became.

Pausing, she set down on the steps of a small shack. Setting her gun to the side, she slid off her pack and pulled out what was left of the food from the grotto man.

She studied her hands, dirty, scraped, warriors hands. Hands that have dealt and taken punishment. She scanned the hill and the other shacks, rubbed her eye with the back of her hand, wincing at the bruise on her cheek. She was tired. Of everything. There had to be a better way. If all this was something once, why couldn't it be again? The areas of lush overgrowth, the bay, the grotto all suggested that it could. It was possible.

As she gnawed on dried meat, she heard the weeds rustle to her right along the edge of the shack. Jumping to her feet, her gun instantly up in front of her, the reeds shook, parted, and two dogs slipped out of the brush. Both froze when the saw her, hackles up, but sniffed the air of the dried fish from her bag.

Alice eyed them both, standing firmly between herself and her pack, but then recognized one to be the dog from the bus.

"Hey...I know you..." She cautiously lowered her gun, tucking it under her arm as she reached for the pouch with the dried fish. Both dogs perked, their eyes softening, but hackles remained raised and tails down -- guarded.

She pulled a few pieces from the pouch and extended her hand. The dog from the bus tipped his head, his gaze flicking between her and the meat. He took a tentative step forward, but the dog instantly pulled back.

"Okay. No problem," Alice said, and simply tossed the pieces of fish to the ground.

Both dogs snapped them up in one swallow.

Looking into the pouch, she realized there was barely any left and she hadn't eaten much. She had shared what she could.

"Sorry guys, that's it. I need to eat, too." She smiled, and the dog from the bus wagged his tail. Alice thought maybe she'd made a friend or two, thought that might not be a bad thing, but when she turned to sit down again, setting her rifle near her bag, the bus dog bristled, a growl growing in his throat. He took two steps toward her.

Turning toward them both, but stepping back and away, she eyed them as they lowered their stance and moved toward her. Their eyes were on her food pouch.

Her gun was on the steps. This small creature moving toward her through the overgrown grass made her throat clench. He was hungry, like her. He was afraid, like her. She couldn't bring herself to reach for her gun.

Instead, she held the pouch with the remainder of the meat over her head. The dog followed it with his gaze, and Alice pulled back and hurled it as far as she could into the field.

The dogs took off after it, and Alice grabbed her things and slipped between and behind the shacks. She'd have to find more food. Time to hunt, she figured.

With one last glance toward the field, the dogs long gone, she realized there's little room for friendship in desperation.

Continuing a short way through the reeds and a swath of dense trees, Alice climbed a small rise toward the river. At its top, she froze. The landscape curved and opened up, affording her a sweeping view of one section of the wide river. Across the hills and bits of broken cityscape, she could now see a large bridge spanning the water's breadth. On the other side loomed a large cascade of damaged buildings and rising smokestacks set behind an enormous wall that rose against the horizon like a shattered, metallic kingdom.

Crimsa, Alice thought to herself.

Her muscles tensed and a chill ran through the sweat dripping down her back. She tightened her backpack and checked her shotgun.

She stood a moment, unable to move, the monoliths of brick and steel appearing so unexpectedly in the distance unreal and threatening. The air hummed with the dull sound of machinery, the smokestacks tossing acrid clouds into the already putrid sky.

A sound nearby drew her attention and she realized the train tracks ran beside the river and behind a string of old structures. She could hear a rattle making its way toward her and turning, she saw it -- two carts hitched together, their bins piled with sacks of whatever came out of the grotto.

As they approached she kept pace, and when they reached her, she jumped aboard, assuming they'd lead in the general direction Bolain had gone. His father said he was heading back to Crimsa's, and if the sacks were full of metallic rock, then so were the carts.

As she rode along, an immense bridge ahead of her in the distance, and Crimsa's barricaded, rusted-out palace across the river loomed into further into view.

But it was what she saw beneath the bridge on the near side that caught Alice's eye. Filling the expanse from the woods inland out to the river were colorful tents and makeshift structures of corrugated metal and stacked stone blocks, and along the river itself, patched up buildings of brick and stone. Misshapen, and cobbled together, they were far from what they used to be, but nevertheless -- with windows covered by tarps and cloth, doors fashioned from pieces of vehicles, or broken bits of wood -- they offered shelter -- homes, even -- for those within.

On the green, beyond a large banner that read, "Borough Groves", she realized the tents and wooden structures were connected, often creating roomy, sizeable spaces. Outside each, she noticed fire pits, storage bins, and a large tank on stilts with pipes leading down to a pump. From the back of the tank, enormous, ducts ran up alongside the bridge, over the river, to the elusive kingdom beyond.

Water.

It was all such a stark contrast to the wildness and desolation she'd been through and around so far; in spite of the damaged buildings, and broken structures around her, those living here had clearly made it home.

As much as her own abandoned-neighborhood settlement was home for her.

Her heart squeezed at the thought.

She rode along, watching the sludge-filled river shove its way along beside her and had a moment of sadness, fear, wondering how her neighbors were faring; wondering if she'd ever make it back to them. *Lily...*

Instinctively she gripped the strap on her pack, tapping the pocket with her sister's meds, keeping her bounty close.

As the bridge drew closer, she could see that the tracks curved behind the buildings and stretched across the river beneath it, vanishing into a hole in the side of the surrounding wall.

She also saw guards. A group of them walking along the river's edge.

She leapt off the carts and headed for the underbrush, running down an embankment away from the river.

At the bottom, she chanced a look out and back, up toward the direction she came. The guards were either behind the buildings or took the carts across the river -- Alice assumed the latter as they were probably there to ensure their safe arrival and that no hitchhikers were on board.

She slipped from the trees and ran behind a shed, quietly making her way around it to get a better look at the Grove and where she was.

As she considered what to do next her attention turned to a gaggle of children who erupted out of one of the brick buildings, laughing and tossing a small, weighted sack between them. They tumbled down the slope to the flats below.

They noticed her and stopped short, their sudden silence drawing the attention of a few adults who were outside stacking wood, or pumping water.

Two older men sitting on a wooden bench rose and made their way toward her.

They were identical, and each wore robes and a tunic, but the colors were opposite: blue tunic and cream robe on one, cream tunic and blue robe on the other.

Their round faces flushed red as they blustered over to her, both speaking at once, one over the other.

"Hello traveler -- "

"Hello hello -- "

"This is Dean," said one, motioning to his twin.

"And this is Drummond," offered the other.

"You must be the one -- "

"Who set off the alarm -- "

"Created quite a stir around here -- "

"And unfortunately had guards swarming everywhere…"

Their arms were a blur of motion as they spoke over one another; each threatening to collide with the other as they walked, talked, and gesticulated. They were comical and odd and a little overwhelming. She wasn't sure if their approach was genuinely welcoming, or a clever misdirection. She was not entirely trustful. Not anymore.

When they finally reached where Alice stood, her posture remained stiff and defensive. She glanced over their shoulders where others had gathered to take notice.

They reached their arms out toward her, but she backed away, grabbing at her weapon.

The rotund men put up their hands, their faces and manner flapping and apologetic.

"Oh no need for that -- "

"No, no…just welcoming you…"

"We don't get many travelers…."

"*Any*, actually…"

A woman appeared behind them then, parting them like curtains and stepping between them.

"For crying out loud, don't suffocate her."

She shooed them away and smiled at Alice, extending an arm to invite her to follow.

Casting a quick glance to the blustery duo, Alice gingerly followed behind the woman, never quite taking her eye from all the activity surrounding them.

"Don't mind them. The Downer is a place of routine, every day like the next. And while once it was fairly united, people traveling about, it has become fractured, everyone cautious, keeping to themselves and wary of others. We aren't even sure what, if anything, exists beyond our small enclave anymore.

"For them to see a wanderer is like getting a present. Breaks up the dreariness of our days."

The woman was gentle, easy, inviting, her hair caught and wrapped in a soft, woven scarf on her head, her skin dark and a bit weathered.

"You appear to have traveled quite a ways. Perhaps you'd like to clean up a bit?"

Alice dipped her head and ran her hand through her hair. She thought of the muddy pond (which felt like a lifetime ago), the tussle with the guards, the cut on her temple, chasing the boy through the grotto -- she realized she must look a mess.

Then again, it's been a rough trip.

While a chance to finally clean up and take a break sounded like a dream, there was no way to tell if this woman was more like the grotto man or Duchess; was she genuinely gracious, or deceptive?

Alice took a moment to glance around. She locked eyes with the woman, making it clear she was not afraid of her, that she could hold her own. She stood tall, squared her shoulders, made an obvious adjustment to the strap of her shotgun-axe.

When she spoke it was flat, noncommittal. "Sure, that would be great. Thanks."

The woman never gave her name, didn't speak much beyond what was necessary, always smiling kindly. Guiding her into a small tent, she tried to take Alice's gear, just to set it aside, but Alice clung to both, snatching them back from the woman's hands, and so the woman just nodded toward a simple basin with water and left her.

Once alone, Alice glanced around her -- a quick check for anyone hidden, waiting -- and when certain there was no one, she placed her gear in front her on the floor between herself and the basin.

A cloth hung on the wall nearby. Soaking it, she gently wiped around the bruises and scrapes on her face. Then she tipped her head forward, scooping her hands in the water and pouring it through her hair.

Finally, she scrubbed her hands and arms, watching the water turn the same murky color of the sky.

When done, she picked up her gear and turned toward the room again, scanning the cushions and blankets, rough wooden shelves and hooks on the walls holding shirts, shawls, other clothing. Colorful tarps divided spaces where there weren't walls to do so, creating hallways, rooms of yellows, corals, blues -- colors Alice assumed used to fill the world outside. She wondered how they made so many colors, how they created dyes and tints. The sun slipping through small openings cast dappled, diffused light throughout, while small lanterns sat on tables ready for when the sun went down.

While nothing there was really better than anything she owned back home, and even though it sat in the shadow of Crimsa's noisy, ominous citadel, those who lived there had worked hard to make it comfortable, welcoming...to make it a home.

When she reemerged, cleaner, scrapes tended to and feeling a little more human, it had grown dark, and the fires were lit along the green.

Alice moved about, winding in and around the fire pits, not wanting to intrude on family evenings, but suddenly feeling just a little bit homesick. She had no idea just how far from home she was, or where she'd find herself if -- *when* -- she got back through the Breach. She also had no idea how *long* she'd been gone. She had lost all track of time, and running from the Rookers, tumbling through the doorway -- it all felt like a lifetime ago. She felt a pit in her stomach, her heart tightening in her chest. She could come back to a decimated neighborhood and everyone gone.

The bumbling duo who had nearly run her over when she first ventured out of the woods waved her over to their little bench where they now sat, a small fire before them, and warm bowls of stew cupped in their hands.

She nearly pretended she didn't see them, but the smells wafting together as everyone had their meals made her heady and hungry. So she skulked tentatively over, keeping her guard up and her belongings close and pulled up a simple, wooden stool.

A small cadre of children appeared and huddled around her on the ground. They peered at her, at her things; they chattered to one another, then got shy if she met their gaze.

Alice smiled at them. Most were about the same age as Lily. Their hands and face were dirty, clothes stained with what appeared to be the slimy muck from the river. None too young to work, she supposed.

"Hello," she said softly, treating them like timid animals who might frighten at a sudden, loud noise.

None of them spoke with her. They looked to one another and back to her full of obvious curiosity, but without ever asking a question.

Within a few moments, a few adults carefully herded them away, uncertain glances cast toward Alice.

The clouds overhead remained but had yet to let loose with any rain. They did, however, make the night inky black. Had it not been for the apparently eternal glow from hulking buildings looming across the river, it would have been impossible to see.

Turning back to the duo on the bench, she accepted a bowl of stew and a hunk of warm, soft bread that was offered to her.

"Thank you…" she said.

Dean and Drummond smiled in unison and exchanged a look.

"So…" Dean began, clearly the one more comfortable with beginning conversations, "How, exactly, did you end up here?"

"And why?" added Drummond quickly.

Alice eyed them both. Everyone who asked that question seemed to be hoping for a particular answer, but she wasn't sure what that was.

"It...it was an accident. I was being chased, and the only escape I had was --"

Again, the two men exchanged a look, this one puzzled, expectant.

"Yes?"

"How did you escape?"

Alice realized maybe she shouldn't have said anything. No one is supposed to be able to leave The Downer, apparently, and she doesn't want Bolain in any more trouble.

She shook her head. "I fell through a hole in the Breach, I guess. A weak point, or broken gate. I don't really know because it happened so fast. I stumbled, and the next thing I knew I was sliding down a muddy slope into a pond."

She lowered her head to her bowl and continued eating, ignoring the fact that Dean and Drummond remained paused, staring, clearly hoping for me.

Alice ate quickly, getting through the meal without any more conversation. She concentrated on the food, which was the closest thing to home she'd had thus far, and tried to make it clear with a stony silence that she had nothing else to say.

Instead, she settled for the occasional grateful smile toward her hosts, a brief, "Thank you. That was delicious," and then quietly excused herself to wander around the area.

She meandered back up the rise toward the building along the river. Where once there had been a road between the green and the buildings, it was now just a stretch of broken concrete reclaimed by nature.

Looking up at the buildings, she could see faint lights and voices coming from windows; more people in one place than she'd seen in a very long time. The sounds rose and fell into the night, occasionally punctuated by a soft trill of laughter, followed by an admonition to settle down.

She couldn't tell if people here were truly content, or had they simply made peace with their situation? Nothing here was truly theirs, even though they had set up a comfortable place for themselves. Throughout it all, she could sense an uneasiness, an understanding that at any moment it could be taken away on a whim.

None of it was theirs, it was -- gifted -- by those who control it, and so it could all disappear without warning.

Turning away from the green she saw a small alleyway running between two of the brick homes. Alice slipped into the shadows there, making her way toward the sound of the river tripping and gurgling around occasional rocks and debris.

The land there dropped sharply, a mix of brush and rocks down to the water below.

Clearly, the only way across was the bridge, and the bridge led straight into Crimsa's fortress.

Following an old walkway behind the buildings and along the tree line, Alice worked her way toward the bridge. Looking up she noticed another camera panning along as she walked. She thought about lifting her rifle and taking it out but thought better of it. Instead, she dropped her gaze and slipped into the shadows beneath the trees.

Reaching the pylons of the bridge, she sank to the ground amid tall grasses and bushes, removing her gear and setting it nearby.

She listened to the breeze in the trees, noticing the sounds wafting from the green had quieted. She needed to get some rest, but she didn't feel entirely comfortable in the settlement. They had been almost too friendly, and that set off a red flag for her. Maybe it was too long living as a Rummie, always looking over her shoulder, forever aware that a Rooker could be close by; that things were not always as they seemed.

Quiet didn't mean safe. It just meant quiet.

As her eyes began to grow heavy, she thought she saw a flash of white on the ramp up to the bridge. But she was tired, it was dark, and she drifted off before giving it much thought.

Unto the Breach

For the second time, Alice woke violently. This time it was to a boot in her gut which doubled her over. Rolling to her side, she went to grab her gun, but it wasn't there.

Catching her breath and opening her eyes, she saw a new faction of guards, three rifles trained on her.

Beyond them, a group of kids tore through her pack, pulling out her flashlight, the empty food basket, the fuel cell.

"Hey! That's my stuff!" Ignoring the weapons surrounding her she lunged toward the kids and her bag, but a pair of boots stepped in front of her, stopping her.

Beyond them, the woman -- her face stoic but somehow sad -- and a guard nearby undoing restraints from a man; dark, dirty, his face scarred and wounded who, upon release, went to the woman and shared an embrace.

Alice realized she'd been traded.

Freaking great. She thought.

"Get up!" The largest of the guards yanked her by the collar and she stumbled to her feet. Another grabbed her hands and bound them behind her. That same guard had her shotgun over his shoulder. He was skinny for a guard, and wouldn't meet her eye when she turned toward him.

Alice looked them all over; yes, they were armored and carried weapons, but beneath their helmets, they didn't appear to be much of anything. Their might was all on the outside.

The Rookers were more frightening.

For a half second, she considered escaping; she thought she could take out the one behind her, run under the bridge ramp, and disappear in the overgrowth beneath.

But then she realized -- this would get her into the compound. No finding a way through gates, or security...right in through the front door.

After that, well, she didn't know. But her whole life was like that, wasn't it? Everything was one step at a time.

Scowling at the kids rummaging through her pack, she took a few threatening stomps toward them. While they scampered a few feet away, the guards yanked her back, and they returned to emptying every compartment, strewing the contents on the ground.

What was garbage and playthings to them, was gold to her.

It was *life* to Lily.

Now it was gone.

Lily. Something still nagged at her and every time she thought of her sister she felt heady, clouded, unable to focus.

And angry. A scarlet rage that coursed through her veins like blood.

Alice fought against her captures, lunging again toward the children, the guard's hold barely restraining her. "Goddammit! That's mine! That's MINE! I need the meds in there! Fuck!"

She yanked as hard as she could, thrashing, breaking free of the guard's grip and stumbling toward the children, her pack, and the woman -- whose shameful gaze lowered to the ground.

"Please..." Alice tried lowering her voice to appeal to them peacefully. "My sister needs the meds in the bag. Just those. You can keep everything else."

The guards were on her again, pulling her to her feet, and upon standing she found herself face to face with the woman.

Alice held still, save for continuing to pull forward against her restraints. The woman's eyes grew soft, and she took half a step toward the pack.

A shot rang through the air above their heads causing everyone to freeze. Turning her head, Alice saw one of the guards, his weapon pointed in the air where he had fired a warning shot, his steely gaze trained on the woman.

"I'm sorry..." she breathed, stepping away.

All three guards took hold of Alice and began dragging her away.

"Son of a bitch!" She yelled, the rage of everything suddenly breaking free; she felt no sympathy for the woman's need to trade her life for another's -- the world was tough and there's no room for friendship in desperation.

But Alice was tougher. "I'll come back here! I'll fucking take it all back from you and anything else I feel like grabbing. You think this is over? Guard yourselves well. Your homes, your fucking families...I don't care. I don't know what the world is like for you here, but I know what it's like where I'm from, and I'm used to fighting for what's mine! I'm used to it! Are *you*?" She fixed her gaze on the woman, who stood still, unable to hide her fear.

"ARE YOU?! I'll fucking take it ALL."

Alice spat the last of her words toward everyone in the field. She was done being kind. Done trying to understand. Then, flanked by Crimsa's guards, she was led up the ramp to the bridge.

Once on top she could see the river emptied into a small bay, over which the bridge arched, bits of it rebuilt, reinforced, where it was damaged and decaying. Long, with thick cables strung between metal towers, it stretched out before them like a concrete ribbon, its surface cracked, pocked, broken.

They shoved her forward and began leading her across, the cluster of towers, structures, spires, pipes vents and beams of the compound now clearly in view.

Below, the shoreline was bordered by an enormous stone, wood and steel wall. A patchwork of found material from storefront walls to vehicle pieces, corrugated metal -- anything that would aid in creating a barricade had been meshed together to form the infamous wall. And evenly spaced along its surface -- the spikes of long-told stories, heads of enemies impaled upon them ranging from ancient skulls, the pikes poking up out of eyeholes, to slightly more recent, decaying, with dried blood staining the length of the pole.

At intervals along the wall rose enclosed towers atop which sat horn-shaped speakers. One guard was posted in each tower.

As if on cue, a siren blared, a brief rise and fall, followed by a voice -- resonating, female, manic, "Heads will roll!"

Alice took a steadying breath, walking among her guardian escorts, wondering now if this was such a good idea after all. What if the horror stories were all true? What if this was more than she could handle?

Sometimes a good stealth break-in *was* the better option. But it was too late now -- she was heading in without a weapon, without her pack, just herself and whatever she could manage.

She walked along taking mental note of her guards. One tended to look out down the river, only occasionally checking back on her. Another was small, not much larger than her, slim. The third walked oddly -- a limp? An injury? The slim one had her shotgun; the one who wouldn't look at her as he tied her hands together.

Glancing quickly behind her she met a visor half shielding eyes appeared terrified before they pulled away and looked up over her head toward their destination.

That's when she noticed it -- the collar. Glancing quickly at each guard she could just make out the brass glint, each one wearing the same thing as Bolain. Each one with a set of blinking red lights.

She'd grown up fending off packs of wild dogs, intruders, and even took out three Rookers once on her own. Three, mildly threatening, armored and armed guards shouldn't be much harder, even with a ribcage sore from being kicked.

Usually, she could use the fact that she was a girl to her advantage; opponents almost *always* underestimated her.

As they got closer, she could see the gateway; a double steel door in the fortress wall. No extra guards beyond those in the tower.

She arched her back against her bound arms, checking the rope on her wrists.

When they grabbed her, she squeezed her fists, pressing her knuckles together which forced her wrists apart. In the frenzy of controlling her, the skinny guard who tied her hands hadn't noticed.

Now, as she relaxed, the rope slacked. With a little wiggling, she thought she could slip her hands free.

They had reached the other side of the bridge, the last stretch slanting downward to the embankment.

From there a short run of barren land led up to the compound wall and the steel front door.

Two guards stood in front of her, the third -- with her weapon -- remained behind her to her left. Alice wondered what they were waiting for until she heard the tell-tale click and hum of a camera spinning and adjusting. Glancing up to her left she saw it: small, concealed, but clearly trained on their small party.

The sound of creaks and grinds and rusted metal sliding across itself followed, and slowly the door of the gate cracked open, sliding apart at the center and parting like a curtain.

It opened just wide enough for them to come through two at a time. And so the guards ahead of her stepped through at which point Alice slipped her hands from the rope which dropped to the ground.

The skinny guard behind her glanced down at it, confused, intrigued, as though a pot of gold had fallen from the sky.

In that distracted moment, she whirled, using the flat of her hand on his exposed nose, followed by a sharp snap of her boot to his kneecaps.

He crumbled to the ground like wet paper, her rifle clambering to the pavement.

She dropped down to grab it as the other two whirled at the sound, looking to where she should have been standing, rather than to where she was on the ground, her rifle primed and aimed.

Before they could react she took two shots -- one at each of them. The first hit squarely in his exposed thigh and he, too, went down in a heap. The second nicked the guard's arm causing him to drop his weapon, but he lunged at her, throwing his body forward.

Alice rolled, wielding the axe end of her combo weapon and nearly took his arm clean off. He wailed, grabbing at the half-severed limb, stumbling away, delirious.

Without another thought, she leapt up, grabbing one of their rifles and some ammo, and slid through the small opening of the gate doors, stepping over the guard wedged between them where he lay grasping at the hole in his leg, a dark, red pool growing beneath him.

She was in.

A House of Cards

Alice slung her shotgun-axe over her shoulder, slipped the ammo in her pants pocket, and carried the rifle with both hands.

It took her a moment when she first stepped into the compound to register where she was.

She stood on an open mall, a rail track running to her left, disappearing into the side of a corrugated metal wall.

Directly ahead, the industrial complex rose toward the sky -- a collection of rusted and repurposed buildings. Part of it looked like a factory, other bits were clearly old shipping containers welded together; the front entry was flanked by two old rail cars, positioned almost like stanchions, guardians of the gate, decrepit monuments adorning either side of the gateway into a derelict kingdom.

Three smokestacks of various sizes sat farther back, two silent, empty, one belching brown smoke and ash into the sky, billowing through arcs of spotlights shining upward. To the left, a length of wall extended off the side of the building. Behind it Alice could hear unidentifiable sounds...snorting? Grunting. Things bumping, moving, stomping.

But it was the open space that required a moment to take in. The ground, a mix of cracked stone and dirt, had been raked clean and even.

In its center a circle in the ground in which stood a tree...but not a tree. Made of metal and oxidized to a blue-green, it was comprised of countless bits of scrap; fenders and gears, buckets and tools, all wound together to from the natural twisting and twining of a trunk up into branches...

The branches...like the great draping trees, the branches were formed with varying lengths and widths of chains, all hanging down, reaching for the ground.

It was beautiful.

Alice slowly made her way around the tree, trying to ignore the heartbeat drumming in her ears, and oblivious to the sound of the gates finally grinding shut, the guards left beyond it. Off to the right, beneath a broken elevated walkway to the building, half hidden between collapsed tanks and pieces of furniture, stood a large, glass-enclosed structure, broken panes repaired, some clearly replaced, all held together by iron grid work and inside...

Alice struggled to find her breath. Beyond the glass the inside exploded with color; blooms of deep red and shocking pink erupted from thick, green stems, leaves larger than her palm drooping from their own weight.

She stood peering in, her eyes tripping from plant to plant, each one somehow more colorful than the last. Overhead, a network of tubes led to funnels which in turn dripped a steady stream of water on the plants.

Long planks lined the edges of the space, each loaded with rows of plants Alice recognized: wild carrot, grapes, and some she couldn't identify but that looked just as edible -- a garden of vegetables, fruits and flowers like she had only seen in old, tattered books.

"Oh, Lily..." she breathed, "you would love this."

Continuing around the mall she came upon a small table and chairs -- set out just as if there was a garden party. Sitting on a set of cracked tiles in the ground, weeds pushing up in clusters between them, a small piece of yellow cake sat on a brass plate, along with a bottle of water. As though waiting for someone.

She glanced around but didn't see anyone nearby. Lifting the bottle and holding it to the light, she could the glass was tinted green, making it impossible to tell what the liquid inside might be.

And a closer look at the cake revealed it was moldy, crusted, old.

"I wouldn't if I were you."

Alice whirled around to find Chester standing near the glass flower house.

"Chester! What are you doing here? How -- ?" She glanced around the enclosure looking for how he'd gotten in.

Chester tapped his holo-generator. "Told you. I can zip in and around all I want. Slipped in before the doors shut."

Alice squinted at him, pursing her lips. "You *have* been following me, haven't you?" She wasn't sure if she was angry, disturbed or glad at the idea.

Chester tried to read her face before answering. "Um...maybe?" He opted to neither confirm nor deny.

Alice rolled her eyes. "Would have been nice of you to jump in a few times there. I lost my pack and everything in it!"

Holding his hands in front of him, Chester backed a few steps away, shaking his head. "Nah...I dislike conflict."

Alice sighed. "How convenient."

"However..." Chester held up one finger and stepped sideways, reaching around the corner of the greenhouse. Then he moved forward and lifted his arm in a flourish to reveal --

"My pack!" Alice rushed over to him, accepting the bag from his hand. She dropped to the ground and opened it, rifling through and checking pockets.

"It should all be there," Chester offered. "I made a game of it with the kids and had them run around and see who could retrieve the most." He shifted his weight from foot to foot as he spoke.

Alice pulled out a little plastic container, and in it were the fuel cells she had found. The next pocket over had Lily's meds. "Oh my god, Chester! You. Are. AWESOME! Thank you!" She stepped forward to hug him but he stumbled away, shaking his hands in front of him.

"No, no...that's okay. Thanks. Not a hugger. But -- you are welcome. Besides, now you don't have to go back wreak havoc in the encampment."

Alice stopped and went back to pick up her pack and strap it on. She smiled warmly at him. "Sorry I snapped at you."

Chester waved her away. "Nah...no sweat."

She smiled, then considered Chester a moment -- always drifting in and out, able to build his gizmo to do so... "Chester...if you can build a holo-generator, couldn't you...I mean...why don't you just leave here?"

For the first time ever, Chester's smile faltered -- though only briefly. His eyes crinkled, one corner of his mouth lifting in a half-grin and he shook his head. "Nah. Family and stuff. Can't."

Alice's heart sank. Chester had been a good friend and she wanted to help him. No one who wanted to leave here should have to stay. "Chester...maybe -- "

Again the stomping, snarling, and a sort of deep, throaty barking snort from behind the side wall rumbled through the air.

"What the hell *is* that?" Alice glanced in the direction of the sound.

Chester wrinkled his nose. "Bandeers. Nasty. You don't -- "

Their little reunion was sharply interrupted by an abrupt, and loud, "HEADS WILL ROLL!! I want her head ON A PIKE!" from the parapet sound system, reminding them both where they were.

"That's my cue!" smiled Chester, and fiddling with his wrist he caught her gaze, his grin once again wide and toothy, and slowly, in his fashion, disappeared. "Don't like conflicts..." she heard drifting out before he completely vanished.

Alone again, Alice glanced around. "This is still so strange. Where *is* everyone?" she said to herself. "There has to be more. Something isn't right."

She moved beyond the greenhouse, ducking under the collapsed walkway, following the sounds of machinery. Carefully she stepped over and around buckled walls and support beams. It seemed awfully wrecked and rusted based on what she'd been told. Where was Crimsa's "shining kingdom"? Was *everything* nothing more than stories? Did anyone know the truth?

Moving past two silos she heard the sounds of pumps and hissing, and the air around her grew hot and humid. She found a shed, the door padlocked. Using her axe she broke the lock and pulled the door open on rough, rusted hinges.

Inside she found panels of gauges -- pressure, temperature, pumps -- all connected to pipes and hoses that led out of the shed toward the silos she had passed.

Backtracking, she looked again at the large tanks, realizing the largest pipes led from the silos to the river.

This was processing the water!

But where were the attendants? Why was no one manning the shed, guarding the silos? It was disturbingly empty. Abandoned, even. It didn't make sense.

A sound back toward the shed startled her and she ducked into a crevice between warped walls. But there was nothing. Perhaps just a rodent, something scurrying in and around the debris.

But then she saw someone. One person, bedraggled, tired, trudging between the buildings and around toward the back where they eventually disappeared around a corner.

Carefully, she made her way back toward the greenhouse and the main courtyard and ventured slowly toward the steps of the central building, scanning her surroundings as she went.

She couldn't shake the odd sense surrounding the desolation of the place. Where was the multitude of guards? Where was the faculty of people needed to run a place like this?

She moved closer to one of the railcars flanking the doorway to the enormous main building, which lay open, empty, waiting…

But the moment Alice stepped through, the place erupted in a cacophony of alarms and horns. She spun around to leave, but metal bars dropped from above, blocking the doorway.

Within seconds a small handful of guards appeared in the room surrounding her with the muzzles of multiple types of weapons. One even had a long pole with a spike on the end.

There was nowhere for her to go, that she could see, and with so many weapons mere feet away and pointed straight at her, a fight was out of the question.

Once again she found herself relieved of her possessions.

The guards then stood shoulder to shoulder, a few on either side of her, the tell-tale blood hearts on their battered and rusting armor, the heart scars on their cheekbones, the brass collars around their necks. In spite of their fierce stance and strong display, they all appeared to have seen better days. In spite of the display, their eyes told a wearisome story.

As the alarms died away, their sound was replaced by an enormous racket of clanking machinery and grinding gears. Alice realized it came from a large, central column in the middle of the room that rose up through the ceiling. It rattled, vibrated, sounds of crunching and squealing, and finally a panel slid open revealing an older man. Large, imposing, heavy-set, he filled the tube he'd arrived in, clad in armor similar to that of the guards, although more finished, polished.

His bare arms showed scars of past skirmishes, and while once muscular, had thinned...aged. He wore thick, layered pants and heavy boots that appeared nearly too weighty for him to lift. His hair, gray and long, hung in multiple braids past his shoulders, and he was missing one eye. The other -- startlingly, iridescent blue, the skin at the corners crinkled and papery -- fixed her with a stare that caught her breath.

Her father had had blue eyes like that.

The man strode toward her, exuding a sense of power, but somehow also hinting at age and fatigue, and when he reached her, without a word, he removed her weapon from her, handing it to the guard behind him.

Alice stood tall, unblinking. "So...this your place? I was hoping you might be able to -- "

She wasn't able to finish as the one-eyed man grabbed her by the hair, yanking her head back, his face leaning in close. "I don't care what you hoped. You are an interloper, and will be dealt with as such."

She decided he might not be one to toy with, so she opted for silence, and for waiting to see what might come next.

He roughly released his hold on her and then made a small motion with his head toward the team of guards, spun on his heels, and made his way around the central column and across the room.

The guards immediately closed on Alice, forcing her to follow behind. They moved slowly, passing a hallway on their left down which Alice could see a run of track leading deeper into the facility. At the end a few people moved sacks from carts. While she only counted maybe a half dozen, two stood out. They were somehow familiar. A man and a woman, her hair just to her chin, dirty blonde, tousled in gentle waves, him slight, slim. He turned to the woman beside him, his hand stroking a smudge of dirt from her cheek, touching the brass collar at her neck, and the woman smiled. That smile. It was full, toothy, pushing her cheeks up into her eyes.

Chester.

Family stuff... He had said.

Alice tried to hang back, to get a better look, but the guards pushed her ahead. But she didn't need a better look. She knew who they were.

The guards led her through a darkened hallway at the other end of the room, into another space full of machinery parts, conveyor belts, broken power panels. At the back wall they climbed a twisted, metal staircase.

At the top, they spanned a steel catwalk taking them deeper still into the cavernous ruins, up another platform, and through huge sliding double doors.

There, dim, amber lighting threw odd shadows across the room, but Alice could see it was a kind of atrium. In the center, a single chair faced the back of the room beneath a single bare bulb hanging on a cord from the ceiling.

The far wall remained drenched in darkness, and the whole room smelled of oil and dirt, and things old and decaying.

Alice tried to calm her breathing, but none of this looked particularly welcoming. She considered the fact that she might well be in over her head.

The guards took her to the chair and the old man gestured for her to sit. Once seated, the guards took one step back but remained on the main floor of the atrium, flanking Alice on either side, while the old man moved into the darkness against the wall.

A deafening crack and a crash boomed through the empty space and a series of lights flipped on around the room temporarily blinding Alice.

"Who are you?" The man's voice echoed through the cavernous room.

Alice blinked into the light, waiting for her eyes to adjust; for the spots obscuring her vision to fade.

"I -- well...before we go there, maybe I could ask the same of you? I like to know who I'm talking to."

A flurry of clicks resounded as the guards readied their weapons. But the old man stomped his foot on the ground, the metal beneath his feet ringing with the sound.

When Alice's eyes finally cleared and focused, she saw the old man sink into a kind of rusted, cobbled together throne; scrap metal, machine parts, old weapons welded together into a mishmash seat, the back rising high above his head.

She gasped, as to his right she also saw -- Bolain. He sat, his head tipped, his hands clasped together.

"Leave her be," the man said to the guards, who withdrew their weapons. "It's no matter. She's not long for here anyway. Her head will soon join the others."

He turned his attention back to Alice. "I am Rud. And you are here because you trespassed through the Breach."

Alice's heart galloped in her chest, but she knew that to show that, would be to admit defeat already. Just as with the Rookers, posture, attitude -- it defined the interaction.

She took a breath. Her throat was dry, full of dust and grit. "Well, I would have called ahead, but I didn't know how. Communications these days are so impossible -- "

"ENOUGH!" Rud stomped his booted foot again, causing the steel riser his throne sat on to waver and shudder. Alice saw Bolain grab the arms of his chair.

"Enough," Rud repeated. "You transgressed, you are not welcome, and Crimsa will pass sentence upon you."

"You can't do that yourself? Huh." Alice knew she'd pushed it before the words were out of her mouth, and the staff to the back of her head confirmed it. She grunted at the impact, her vision clouding a moment, a ringing rising in her ears. That was gonna leave an egg.

Rud made a gesture toward Bolain and pushed a button on what appeared to be a small radio on his belt. Bolain stiffened a moment, the lights on his collar growing a steady orange for a brief second, before returning to flashing red. Bolain, once the spasm subsided, scrambled past him to the wall on his left and pulled a lever on panel.

The room filled with the same mechanical clanking and banging that Alice heard when Rud arrived in the tube, but this time, from somewhere up above, another throne descended from the inky blackness overhead. Held aloft by massive chains, it lowered slowly, slowly down beside her companion.

Alice's eyes grew wide as the throne settled into place. There, sitting upon it -- or rather, almost *in* it -- was some sort of monstrous amalgamation of woman and machine. Alice couldn't tell where one ended and the other began, nor if the part that was woman was even still actually alive in any way.

She was not so much sitting on the throne as she nearly *was* the throne, with parts and bits of human body in and about the metal. Her head, the most complete human part of her, perched stiffly on metal shoulders, one eye made of goggle bits, her mouth obscured by a kind of mesh with cables running down and disappearing behind her. Around her neck, a dried, desiccated heart hung on a heavy cord.

Her one eye blinked, although even that appeared automatic, practiced. She raised her head, training her gaze on Alice, her eye narrowing, accusing. She stiffly banged her hand on the arm of her throne, causing it to rattle.

Alice wasn't sure how much of Crimsa was human at all.

Crimsa lifted her arm, pointing her metallic finger in Alice's direction as the sudden sound of a suction pump was followed by the familiar female voice, "Heads Will Roll!" reverberating around the room.

It was quickly followed by "Trespasser! You have invaded The Downer and will now face sentencing..."

In the pause that followed Alice interjected, her head beginning to throb. "Honestly, it was an accident. I had no desire to be here, and all I'd like to do is leave..."

"Trespasser!" Crimsa's voice boomed again. "You are guilty! You are an enemy of the court and shall be dealt with as an aggressor!"

Alice glanced at Bolain, who stood cowering by the lever. The sound of suction pumps and mechanics continued and Alice couldn't shake the feeling that something was very, very off.

She glanced at the guards out of the corner of her eye and caught more than one of them looking down, or away. She also noticed that several of the guns were actually missing magazines.

They were empty!

How had she missed that?

She looked to Rud who simply sat, stoic, but looking more and more like it was forced. Studied. A performance for a small, captive audience.

Again Alice glanced at the guards, at the weapons, and she noticed several of them looking uncertain, their posture weakening.

Looking back to Crimsa, she sat unmoving, quiet, save for the suction pumps and forced air.

And it hit Alice harder than the staff to her head -- it's all *fake*. This was all there was of Crimsa's kingdom...all that was left.

The same passage of time that laid claim to the buildings and streets had finally taken its toll on the Clan of Crimsa. They were hanging onto power with smoke and mirrors.

She started laughing, causing the guards to startle and step back, and Bolain to freeze against the wall, while Crimsa's voice shuttered mechanically through the space, "Silence! Or Heads. Will. Roll!"

Rud glared with his one, ice blue eye, but he remained seated, simply stomping his boots on the metal platform which rattled and shook and threatened to dislodge from the wall.

Alice scanned them all: Rud and his feigned powerful posturing, Crimsa and her mashed together mechanical humanity seemingly restricted to her metallic throne, and the guards -- frail, afraid, with little to defend themselves, let alone launch an attack.

Bluster, shouting, posing and posturing...but nothing more.

Crimsa's voice, the rhythm of the pumps, Rud's boots all echoed and ricocheted around the space, but that just made Alice laugh even harder -- her voice rising to meet the echoed bouncing, squeaking, whining of the flimsy, rusting, decaying steel all around them.

"Silence!" Rud bellowed, but without much conviction, it seemed to Alice.

It was all just a house of cards.

Falling Down

The rumbling through the space continued to grow, Rud's rage increasing, but clearly without the power or strength to truly do anything about it. He was without the resources, strength -- maybe even courage -- to do anything more than put on a show.

It was all a façade.

Crimsa seemed stuck on repeat, crying out, "Trespasser! Her head on a pike!", and the guards looked about desperately, uncertain what they should be doing. In fact, they all looked like they'd like to run -- like they'd welcome a way out.

Rud jammed his finger down on another button on the controller and all the guards tensed for an instant in response.

Alice seized the moment of confusion to lurch toward the guard with her shotgun, easily connecting with a left hook, and snatching it out of his hands. His helmet clattered off his head to the floor and he scrambled away after it.

Then she spun and kicked out toward the guard holding the pike, his knee snapping, the pole clanging to the ground, rolling away into the shadow beneath the overhang, as he collapsed to the ground gripping his shattered kneecap.

The others instantly broke ranks and stumbled, Crimsa continued her auto-repeat, and Rud's voice thundered, "Apprehend her!"

Rolling to the side, Alice heard the one gun that had ammunition fire, followed by a loud ping and a roar from Rud.

Glancing up to his throne, Alice saw him grab a spot on his upper chest and slip from his chair. The shot ricocheted off the steel beams and hit him instead.

Alice took aim and fired, dropping the guard who had missed his shot. Now all the guards completely scattered, and Alice scrambled to her feet, grabbing up her pack and heading for the door.

"Bolain!" she called, motioning for him to follow her.

The boy stood frozen in panic a moment, waiting for an electronic jolt that didn't come, then reached for the cable and tubes around Crimsa's throne. With one, forceful yank, he pulled several of them free releasing sparks and steam, and a horrific wail from Crimsa, herself.

The lights on his collar went dead.

While Rud made a half-hearted lurch toward him, the shot in his chest proved a critical wound and he stumbled. Bolain easily slipped away from him, scrambling down to Alice below.

Alice grabbed his hand, and they ran.

Behind them, the handful of guards fell into complete disarray as Rud screamed orders at them while stumbling about the rickety platform. Slowly Alice heard the tell-tale creak and whine of bolts snapping, metal bending, and amid a few panicked gunshots, the guards fled in all directions within the atrium, while Alice and Bolain headed for the exit.

Behind them, the sounds of collapsing metal and snapping pipes squealed through the air as well as the panicked cries of guards. Behind it all, they heard Crimsa's slowly failing refrain, "Stop...her...or... heads...will..." trailing down in pitch, mechanics failing.

Once back in the main entry hall, Alice turned to see the catwalk and metal stairs give way. Guards were nowhere to be seen, but she could hear their clattering and yelling as they scrambled for their own paths to safety.

Alice and Bolain ran for the door, but Alice stopped at the side hallway.

"Hang on!" she yelled over the rattling chaos behind them and bolted down to the room at the end. There she found the half dozen people -- including the two she knew were Chester's parents -- frozen, gripping rails and sides of carts as the building clanged around them.

They turned to Alice, gaunt, fearful.

"Let's go!" she yelled at them all, motioning for them to follow. No one moved, paralyzed by fear. She looked at the man and woman and reached out her hand.

"Chester's waiting," she pleaded with them. But no one moved.

"Alice!" Bolain called, afraid the guards might still follow, or the building might come down around them.

Alice stood just a moment more, trying to will them to follow. But in the end, she had to leave them. They were too afraid to trust.

"I'll tell him to come get you," she said, and turned back down the hall to Bolain.

At the front entrance, Bolain paused, pulling open a piece of a metal panel from the wall, smashing a few buttons, which in turn raised the metal bars in front of the opening.

Alice smiled through heavy, ragged breaths. "You're the best, Bolain. Let's get out of here."

She paused a moment, glancing at the greenhouse, wanting to stop and grab some of what was in there. They could get some of it to grow back home. But a grinding sound behind them near the side of the compound changed her mind.

Without pause, they raced across the mall together, passed the moldy cake and bottled water, around the metal tree and to the gate.

Again Bolain uncovered a box, this one opening the main gate, and the two fled, passed the now dead guard that had been wedged in the door. Once through, Alice turned, shoving the guard out of the way to try and force the doors closed behind them.

She could still hear clanking and clamoring and the sounds of bending, twisting metal from inside and her gaze flicked quickly toward the main entrance.

Then that sound was joined by something else. A siren, Crimsa's warped and garbled battle cry through the loud speaker, and then the rumbling sound of something approaching; growls and roars came from around the wall causing Alice and Bolain to skid to a stop at the foot of the ramp to the bridge.

Turning, they saw them round the corner -- a pack of beasts like nothing Alice had ever seen. A strange amalgamation of an overgrown bear and a rhino. Dense, dark fur covered their heads, snouts and longer necks, but grew sparse on their torsos and legs, their feet club-like with three large, hoofed toes. They had small eyes, fierce jaws, and they charged toward the bridge, snarling and snapping.

Alice saw Bolain's eyes grow wide with terror, "Bandeers!" he cried.

"What the hell?" Alice grabbed him by the arm and pulled him to running. They took off across the bridge, the settlement below full of people pointing and yelling.

They ran hard, the Bandeers now at the top of the ramp, their hooves thundering on the concrete, causing deeper cracks, furrows and bits of stone to fly off.

Alice chanced a look back -- they were gaining -- but she wondered if the bridge might actually begin to give way.

With no time to see, the two barreled ahead reaching the other side of the bridge and skidding down the far ramp.

Bolain tripped and fell, crying out as his leg scraped along the ground. Alice slid to a stop, ran back up and helped him to his feet.

In that moment she also turned, and shoving Bolain behind her, grabbed her shotgun and fired: Once. Twice.

One beast stumbled, tumbled and slid to a halt, dead. Another plowed into it, tripping, falling, hitting the ground with a thud. But four more continued on, their bellowing echoing through the air.

Closer.

Alice snatched Bolain and they ran the rest of the way down the ramp, making a sharp turn into some brush at the bottom. People in the settlements now scattered, screaming, as the Bandeers skid to a halt halfway down the ramp, sniffing the air around them.

Bolain peered through a tangle of branches, keeping low, out of sight. The Bandeers stood still, noses to the sky, tongues flicking, tasting the air around them. "They have terrible eyesight," explained Bolain, keeping his voice low, soft. "So they sniff for scents with their nose and their tongues."

Alice peered out as well, then whispered, "We need to get to the Breach and get out. Do you have your -- thing?"

Bolain looked down and pulled at the cord around his neck, lifting it up out of his shirt and over his head, handing it to Alice. "Here, you take it. I have to go home. I can't leave them."

Alice heard the Bandeers making a slow descent down the ramp, huffing, and snorting like bulls. Like the Rookers, they seemed to like to take their time with the kill.

She looked at him, "We can come back and get them. With help."

Bolain shook his head. "*You* do that then..." He lowered his gaze, taking a deep breath. When he looked back up at her, his eyes full of frightened tears, for the first time he looked like the child he was -- alone, missing his family. "I want to go home."

Alice sighed and placed her hand on his head. "Okay. That's okay." She touched the brass collar around his neck.

"I wish I could get that off for you..."

Bolain shook his head. "My dad will get it."

Alice smiled at him. "Okay, then I'll get the -- Bandeers? -- to follow me, and you head home. Okay?"

Bolain only nodded. Alice knelt down in front of him. "Thank you. And your parents were right. You are incredibly brave."

Bolain smiled, wiping away his tears, and explained how to use his Breach breaker. The small screen would tell her which direction to go to find a length of Breach, and then a decoder would unlock the door. "Power's running low, tho," he said as he handed it over to her.

Alice smiled and hugged him. Feeling his smallness, and in that, realized how much she missed Lily. Her vision wavered a moment and she understood his need to go home.

They could hear the Bandeers on the ground at the base of the bridge. One of them charged into the settlement, tossing aside tables and tents, adults grabbing children and racing into the woods for cover. The others remained, a few yards away, pawing at the ground, throwing their heads around, pausing once or twice to catch a scent on the breeze.

It was time to go.

"Okay," Alice said. " You ready?"

Bolain nodded.

Alice put the breaker around her neck, checking the direction to run, and lifted her shotgun.

She looked once more at Bolain and smiled gently. She needed to give him every chance of getting out. "Get ready to run."

Bolain nodded.

Then she burst from the bushes, howling and screeching, and as soon as she bolted the three Bandeers at the foot of the bridge lifted their heads, gave a growling, snorting, barking snarl and took off after her.

As soon as the beasts had passed, Bolain slipped from the brush and with one, last, glance backward, took off in the opposite direction -- home.

Alice tripped, slipped, skid and ran across rough, broken, tangled terrain. She changed her direction, zigzagging into and out of trees, over and around foundations, rubble, and debris.

The Bandeers followed, but they were big, heavy, lumbering -- although they made up for some of it in steady footing. Rarely did they stumble or slip.

Checking the gizmo around her neck she confirmed she was headed in the right direction, the little, green radar light flashing repeatedly. It wasn't that far.

She tossed a glance behind her.

Neither were the Bandeers. They were ugly, ferocious, and apparently did not tire.

At the top of a small rise stood a partial wall. She dove behind it and checked her shotgun. One shot loaded, and two bullets left.

Peering around the edge of the wall, she saw the Bandeers about halfway up, again, pausing to check the air for her scent. Behind them and over the rise, Crimsa's citadel shuddered, parts of the structure threatening to fail and sending a rumble through the ground that the Bandeers braced against.

Alice took a deep breath, sliding the muzzle of her gun out around the wall, taking aim, and --

She hit one of the beasts square in the forehead and it went down in a heap.

The remaining two let loose with deafening, blasting howls, and took off toward her.

She jumped up and ran, tumbling once over the lip of another wall hidden in brush, coming down hard on her side. Scrambling, she pushed on, the pain in her rib sharp, but the beasts behind her all the motivation she needed to force her way past it.

The light on Bolain's gadget grew bigger, blinking brighter, and Alice realized that the Breach should come into view when she rounded the corner up a hill.

Sure enough, as she wound her way up the incline, weaving between buildings and scattered debris, she saw it. It was just on the other side of a large, flat bottomed, concrete culvert a few yards ahead. Off in the distance, she spotted a pylon -- one of the relays placed sporadically along the border that anchored and activated the electric doors and security charge for the Breach.

To her right, just past the culvert, was the ravine she had first tumbled into.

Somehow she'd come full circle. But that was still far off. The Breach breaker suggested an exit straight across, past some broken piles of concrete -- maybe through the thin stand of low trees and scraggly brush.

Another rumble in the ground and a quick glance behind her showed a small plume of gray smoke rising up behind the trees.

She took a deep breath, ignoring the stabbing in her side, and forced a burst of speed. Sliding on her heels and backside over the pebbles and dirt that covered the broken concrete walls of the gulley, Alice raced across the bottom toward the small copse of trees against the far hill.

Her breathing came brusque and short, and sweat dripped into her eyes, as she raised the breaker in the direction of the trees. The radar dot flashed, indicating something nearby, causing Alice to pause. Something was right in the area, but she couldn't pinpoint where. She held the Breaker in front of her, but it flickered, as the power threatened to die.

Then she saw him. Chester. Coming into view to her right on the lower branches of a tree. Just as he had when she first met him. He grinned, as though all of this was no more than a game that he continued to thoroughly enjoy. "Go!" he yelled to her.

With a quick glance behind her, she saw the Bandeers skidding down the far side of the gulley.

She stopped, catching Chester's eye. "I don't know where!"

"It's straight ahead and up this first incline…go!

Alice started, then stopped again. "You're parents are there, Chester!" She called to him. "I couldn't get them to come. But go get them -- there's nothing there to stop you anymore!"

Chester froze a moment, the smile fading for the first time.

Alice looked back, the Bandeers now thundering across the bottom of the culvert.

"They're--they're alive?" he stammered.

Now Alice smiled, glad she confirmed her suspicions of who they were. "Yeah, Chester. And Crimsa's nothing. She's gone. Just…just use your gizmo there and go get them."

Chester's grin returned, mixing with a few tears as the Bandeers skid around some broken chunks of concrete, colliding with one another causing a moment of infighting.

"Go, Alice...I got this."

"Thought you didn't like confrontations..."

Chester smiled. "I got *this* one." He glanced at the Bandeers who had paused again to sniff the air overhead.

Nodding, Alice ran, looking back once toward Chester to see him jumping from the tree to the clearing and shouting to distract the Bandeers in his direction, all the while keeping one hand on his holo-generator.

She banged Bolain's gadget on her hand and held it in front of her as she saw Bolain do that first day. It sprang to life as she scrambled up the short hill, pointing to her left beside a stubby, prickly evergreen bush as she reached a plateau. Shoving branches aside, she found an abandoned shipping container half buried in the side of the hill, the opening behind a rotting piece of board.

Alice chanced one, last glance down toward Chester, who she could just barely see was on the ground and grinning wildly at her, his eyes twinkling with defiance. He nodded to her, motioning to the tunnel as the Bandeers began their final, thundering run toward them both.

She waved to him, hoping he'd stay safe, and bolted into the darkness.

Within a few steps the blackness overtook her and she had to stop a moment to fish for her flashlight. This tunnel had no illumination at all and her own light fell weakly into the gloom, leaving swaths of shadowed ground. But she pressed ahead, feeling the earth angle slightly downward.

She moved the best she could in the dark, occasionally stumbling into the rough walls. She couldn't determine the shape of the tunnel -- whether it was straight or curved -- only that it arched slightly downward.

Behind her she suddenly heard a commotion and feared that one or more of the Bandeers had gotten past Chester, so she started to run, the breaker beginning to flash as the door drew near.

She tripped once, landing hard on her knee, skidding as she descended further, and losing her grip on the flashlight.

"Shit..." she exhaled, trying to catch her breath.

Finding her light she struggled to stand, her ankle sharply complaining. As she got to her feet, a beam of light swung over a rusting, square door in the wall of the tunnel just to her right as the breaker pulsed brightly. Limping forward, the scraping, snorting sounds nearing behind her, the tunnel vibrating, Alice fumbled with the breach breaker against the recessed latch. She heard the telltale crackle of an electrical charge releasing, and the squealing of scraping metal as the sound behind her grew closer, closer...

As Alice's heart thundered in her ears, her ankle throbbing, the latch snapped open. With a deep breath, Alice shoved her shoulder against the heavy metal and she fell through, abruptly rolling down the rest of the incline. The gravel scraped her arm, her weapon clattered to the side, her head clunked several times against hard, dry ground.

"Son of a bitch!" she mumbled as she came to a stop at the bottom, her breath sharp and painful. She tried to roll over, to find her weapon, to see where she was but everything wavered -- blurry, unfamiliar. As she collapsed back on the ground she thought she heard the hissing, clanking sounds of the door reengaging --at least she hoped so -- before her vision tunneled down and she fell unconscious.

The Wondering and The Real

A buzzing sound. A hum. Whirring closer.

Footsteps. Voices.

"Alice! Alice?"

Alice's eyes fluttered slowly open, her eyes dry, unfocused, silhouettes of faces overhead against a dingy, mottled sky.

She took a breath. A stabbing pain in her side caused her to stop. *Hold it. Let it out in a slow, easy stream.*

She tried to move her head. It hurt. "Mm..umm…" she tried. Everything ached.

"Shh…Alice. We're here. We've got you. We're going to get you home."

Things came clearer -- her vision, her thoughts. "Shit."

Alice struggled to push up on her elbow. She didn't feel her pack. She flailed a moment, ignoring the stinging points of pain throughout her body.

"My pack...my...Lily's meds..." she coughed. Her throat was dry. She tasted blood. A hand came forward with a water pouch, and as her vision finally cleared, she looked up to see Ryan, another Rummie. "Ryan?"

He smiled. "Yeah. I'm here. So is -- " she watched him exchange a curious look with the others. "So is... everything else you found."

"The meds? Do you have Lily's meds?" She grabbed around the ground near her.

Again an exchange of quiet looks, before Ryan put his hand on her shoulder. "Yeah, Alice. It's good."

Alice relaxed a moment, steadying her breathing.

Ryan wiped some blood and sweat from her head. "Jeez, you scared us."

"What? Why? What's going on?" She wanted to stand, but her legs felt like boulders, and every movement brought a stabbing wave of pain.

Someone helped her sit up. There were three other people from her settlement there and her dirt bike was on the ground near Ryan. Her head pounded. She wasn't where she remembered landing, and if she tried hard to focus she could dimly recall trying to start back toward The Gardens...apparently she didn't make it.

"Just take it easy," said Ryan. "We were attacked by Rookers. Do you remember? Jae -- " he dropped his gaze. "Jae didn't make it. Then they took after you. You went over the edge of a ravine as you took one of them out -- which was seriously awesome, by the way -- but...

"Well, Mallory and I took care of the others. But you went down hard We actually thought that was it for you. That we'd find you in a twisted heap.

"But by the time we reached the ditch you weren't there, and we figured you dodged into the brush. We managed to fend off the other Rookers, and then spent the last day and half looking for you. You're tracker was active but we couldn't get a fix on it. It must have gotten pretty banged up -- the signal kept coming in and out. We almost gave up..."

Alice swallowed. "No...it was the Breach. I -- " she had a hard time concentrating. The pounding in her head distracted her. Sarah Hammond was gently scurrying around her, bandaging wounds, gathering her things.

Ryan put his hand on her arm. "You're alright. We're going to get you home."

They were trying to help her up. To get her on the back of a small trailer hitched to the only quad their settlement had.

Alice fought them. "No --" she pointed behind her, back where she wandered from. "The Breach. I went through…The Downer. It's not what we think, Ryan…there's stuff there…water, plants… This kid, Bolain…" she held up the Breach breaker around her neck. It was smashed, the screen shattered, the button missing. "He gave me this. To get out. And Crimsa…she…"

Her heart started racing, her breathing grew sharp and shallow, her mind swam with too many thoughts. Something wasn't right. This wasn't right.

Ryan tried to calm her, laying his hand on her arm. He picked up the gadget and held it. "What is this? It's cool looking. Bummer it's smashed but I'm sure we can use some of the components. As usual, you made some great finds."

Someone tapped him on the arm. "We should get going," they said to him. It was Frankie, one of the other Rummies.

"No. Stop!" Alice forced the words out, wincing, coughing, pulling Ryan to sit beside her on the trailer.

"Ryan -- I went through the Breach. I followed a boy…a young boy who used *this* -- " She again lifted the gadget around her neck. "It's not what anyone thinks it is, Ryan. I'm telling you. It could change everything..." She fought tears, seeing the faces around her so still, exchanging worried glances.

"Alice -- you put up a good fight with the Rookers, and you took a helluva fall -- " He paused a moment before continuing.

"We knew it was probably too soon for you to be out. That maybe -- "

"No! Ryan -- it's this...*this* -- I promised. I *promised* Bolain I'd help. And there are so many -- " She stopped short and looked her friend in the eye.

"Wait...what do you mean too soon for me to be out?"

Ryan faltered and Mallory stepped forward, sitting beside her. "What do you remember, Alice? Before we set out for the scavenge?"

Alice searched her face, her brow furrowed, her brain feeling foggy and heavy -- and not from the multitude of injuries.

"What...what do you mean?"

Now Sarah moved in, kneeling in front of her. "The Rooker attack several days ago, Alice. You were out on a scavenge run because they raided the settlement..."

Alice had trouble breathing, her vision tunneling down, their voices melding into a strange hum.

She saw herself tipping over the edge of the roof onto the Rooker at Hellerman's house. She took him out without a fight...

Her stomach turned on itself and she gripped the edge of the trailer.

"Alice?"

She stared at Ryan, his face swimming in a rippling pool before her.

Alice saw herself standing over the dead Rooker, the sounds of skirmishes filling the air, gunfire and yelling.

The bushes behind her...

The bushes behind her rustled.

A child Rooker rushed from the shadows.

A child.

She raised her shotgun as Hellerman screamed her name...

The memory swam into view. "I shot...I shot a kid. The Rookers bring their kids and I killed one..."

She remembered feeling sick, the world turning black. Always knowing it was a possibility, she had steeled herself to be able to take out any Rookers that attacked -- even a child.

But when the moment came...when the moment came it didn't matter that it was a child trained to attack, to steal -- to kill.

She was a *child*. And Alice recalled her eyes -- open, unseeing, a doll's eyes reflecting the sun, the life in them gone.

She recalled...

Alice leapt from the trailer, her hands gripping the side of her head, which felt like it might implode. She fell to her knees, retching, struggling for breath.

Oh god...

Ryan was at her side when the memory came clear. He put his arms around her shoulders and held her tight.

Lily.

It was a child -- but not a Rooker.

It was a girl. Running toward the only family she had left amidst the sounds of attack that brought her nothing but night-terrors.

LILY!

Choking on her horror, tears mixing with blood and spit, she sucked in a breath as she remembered.

"RaaaaAAAHHHHH!!" She wrenched herself free of Ryan's hold and stumbled around the field, ignoring the throbbing in her ankle, the pain in her side. "No...nonono...

Her stomach lurched and she fell to her knees retching into the dry, powdered dirt between her hands. Nothing came up, but her body tried anyway, a desperate attempt to purge the horror.

Ryan wandered near, a hand on her shoulder, but the touch woke the beast and Alice jumped again to her feet, fists clenched, face twisted. She pressed the heels of her hands to her eyes and let the hate, and fear, and anger finally take form as she screamed, "AAAHHHHH! I HATE THIS WORLD! I fucking hate it all! I'm so TIRED of FIGHTING!

"Alice -- " Sarah tried to move toward her.

"No! Leave me alone!" Alice stumbled backward, smacking Ryan's hand away as he reached again for her, waving Sarah away. "Oh my god…I killed my sister. I killed my fucking sister!!"

She turned and tripped over a pile of bricks and fell again. She laid on the ground, staring up at the murky yellow sky, the clouds gathering again, threatening rain.

Always rain.

But never green afterward.

Lily.

She was there to protect Lily, and she failed her.

No -- the *world* failed Lily in that it made Alice into a killer.

Alice didn't *fail* her sister. She killed her.

No one starts out their lives a killer.

She killed her thinking she was a Rooker.

Why did she leave the bunker?

Because she was afraid she'd lose what was left of her family.

But she didn't.

Alice did.

Alice lost everything.

She looked up again at the wall, a protruding scar across the landscape.

She thought of Chester and his parents, Bolain and his family.

She thought of everything she saw in the Downer -- plenty of places to live, metallic ore for fuel cells, water to filter, and a compound with plants, processors and more.

She *did* go through and make it out again.

Didn't she?

"I *did* go, Ryan. There are people -- families -- and there are resources that can help us. It's not what everyone thinks..."

More than the stories.

She held the gadget tightly in her hands and held it up to Ryan.

"We have to make this work again. Don't just use its parts. We have to look at it and make it work again. We have to go back, and this wall has to come down. We can't live like this anymore…

I can't -- "

Alice winced and drew a sharp breath. Ryan helped her back up on the trailer and placed his hands over hers.

"Okay. I promise that you and I will take a look at that thing when you are better, okay?"

Alice kept a tight hold on Bolain's Breach breaker as she caught Ryan glancing to the others around them. She knew he was doubtful. They all thought she was crazy with guilt and grief, had tumbled into the gulley, hit her head and imagined it all.

But she'd prove it to them. She'd get the Breach breaker working again and she'd prove it. For Lily -- who would have loved the flowers and the bird with the eye in its tail. For herself, who was tired of scavenging for everything, tired of fighting. Killing. For Chester and Bolain -- living for so long afraid and in hiding -- and all of them.

She'd prove it to them.

Alice Redux

No one starts out life a killer. At least, I don't think so. And even if that's where they end up, maybe there's a way to make it stop.

There has to be a way to make it stop.

The world is black, and gone to shit, and we can't take it back, but maybe we can make it better.

For me it was a now blood-speckled and muddy white rabbit once stuffed beneath a shoulder strap and now clutched in bruised and bloody fingers that says there has to be a way.

Lily.

Sometimes shit happens and it's nothing you can undo, just something you have to live with and it sends you tumbling into a world you never imagined. A world of wilderness and wildness, of rail cars and beasts, pungent tea and warm stew, broken families and gilded queens.

And death.

Sometimes you are forced to see things you cannot unsee and it makes you stand and scream "Enough!"

Make it stop.

Make it better.

For me it was the distant sound of rolling thunder mixing with the echoing screech of Rookers along with the crackling snap of a pylon circuit failing once more that brought dreams of stories told for generations to come; about The Fall, The Downer, a girl named Alice, and the world that came after.

OTHER BOOKS by MELISSA VOLKER

Literary Fiction

Delilah of Sunhats and Swans
Still, Life: a collection of echoes
Where We Go: and other essays & stories

Middle Grade

The Moya Fairwell Series:
The Thirteenth Moon
The A'Chiad

Teen/YA

Anabelle Lost
HIDDEN: an impossible story

please visit her site for more information
www.melissavolker.com

M.Vol

www.ingramcontent.com/pod-product-compliance
Lightning Source LLC
Chambersburg PA
CBHW032212190626
46810CB00019B/2665